Would Beth ha
up towards h
hadn't wanted

Would he have *wanted* to know known what it would be like? If he'd known that the lock would disintegrate on that part of his heart which had been so well protected for so long? That all the old feelings would still be there so completely?

Except they hadn't been complete, had they? Because now he could add the painfully gained wisdom of so many years. And the forgiveness—and the understanding of why it had happened.

His hands held her close; his lips moved over hers so gently. This wasn't about passion— though that was only a heartbeat away. It was about finding a connection again, and asking whether that connection could ever mean enough to make it worth exploring further.

A&E DRAMA

Blood pressure is high and pulses are racing
in these fast-paced dramatic stories from
Mills & Boon® Medical Romance™. They'll move a
mountain to save a life in an emergency, be they the
crash team, emergency doctors, or paramedics.
There are lots of critical engagements amongst
the high tensions and emotional passions in these
exciting stories of lives and loves at risk!

THE SURGEON'S ENGAGEMENT WISH

BY
ALISON ROBERTS

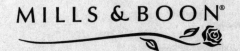

MILLS & BOON®

For Sandra, my friend
in the NZ Department of Conservation
who helped me find out how to save whales. With love.

All the characters in this book have no existence outside the imagination
of the author, and have no relation whatsoever to anyone bearing the
same name or names. They are not even distantly inspired by any
individual known or unknown to the author, and all the incidents are
pure invention.

First published in Great Britain 2005
Paperback edition 2006
Harlequin Mills & Boon Limited,
Eton House, 18-24 Paradise Road, Richmond, Surrey TW9 1SR

© Alison Roberts 2005

ISBN 0 263 84712 8

Set in Times Roman 10½ on 12 pt.
03-0206-47499

Printed and bound in Spain
by Litografia Rosés, S.A., Barcelona

CHAPTER ONE

THE car should *not* have been there.

In the small car park adjacent to the emergency department of Ocean View hospital, yes. In the space reserved for the ambulance, even, if the emergency was dire enough.

But three quarters of the way through the wide electronic doors that led into the reception and triage area?

No *way*!

Nurse Elizabeth Dawson's astonishment rapidly gave way to alarm. The car would have been suspicious enough tucked neatly into an acceptable car-parking slot. An ancient, rusting hulk of a V8. A status symbol amongst the elements of society who preferred to simply ignore any restrictions the law might impose on their lifestyle.

The man climbing out of the driver's seat was even more intimidating. Clad in battered leathers with the 'patch' of his gang emblazoned on the back of the jacket, the heavily tattooed and menacing figure would have alarmed even the most confident of any emergency department staff.

And Beth Dawson was far from the most confident

right now. She had started a new job in a new town only a couple of hours ago, for heaven's sake, and everything was still completely unfamiliar.

No. Not quite everything. The aggression emanating from the gang member she was watching was all *too* familiar.

An unexpected flash of anger cut through her fear. This type of scenario was precisely why she'd left her job in a huge south Auckland hospital so recently. She'd had a gutsful of dealing with violent and uncooperative patients who took any pleasure or even satisfaction out of demonstrating the level of skill she had attained in her chosen profession.

The anger couldn't last long enough to fuel courage, however, given the fact that she was alone in this part of the department. At 1 a.m. in a semi-rural area you wouldn't expect a full waiting room, and the only patient who had come in since midnight was now having his chest pain investigated in one of the two resuscitation rooms.

Beth's finger was pressed firmly against the button summoning assistance and any trace of saliva vanished from her mouth as she watched another two figures emerge from the vehicle. The bizarre sight of the car under the bright lights and filthy tyres on the spotless linoleum had already become just a background to an unpleasant drama unfolding. So had the rhythmic and futile attempts the electronic doors were making to close the small gap left around the obstacle. They touched the rear of the car and then bounced open again. And again.

The movement of the doors did not impede two of the men dragging the final occupant from the rear seat of the car. Little care was afforded the potential injuries of an apparently unconscious victim and a large smear of blood appeared on the pale floor as his feet dragged.

Two more nurses rushed into the space behind Beth, closely followed by the only doctor on duty, Mike Harris. Beth could feel all three of them virtually skidding to a halt as they caught sight of the car inside the building, but she didn't turn her head. Her gaze was fixed on the slumped figure being held up by the armpits. She drew back instinctively as the gang member who had been driving the car started walking towards them.

'Jackal's been shot.'

Beth was aware of broken teeth and the smell of alcohol as the man spoke. She was also quite well aware that the incongruously casual tone of voice was no insurance against the level of implied threat in his next succinct words.

'You'd better *do* something.'

They would be armed, Beth had no doubts about that. There would be knives tucked inside those commando-style boots. At least one of the men was wearing knuckle-dusters and she was quite certain there would be more than one sawn-off shotgun easily accessible in that vehicle.

Her breath escaped in something like a strangled laugh. She had left a big city hospital that had protocols for dealing with precisely this type of incident. Any number of security personnel would be available within seconds and a well-rehearsed police squad only minutes away. And even that kind of back-up hadn't been enough to prevent her best friend, Neroli, giving up her nursing career, having been held at knife point in Beth's old emergency department.

Beth had come to a small-town hospital near the tip

of the south island of New Zealand to find a peaceful place to settle and refocus her life. She had barely begun her first night duty in this tiny emergency department and here she was, facing one of her worst nightmares. A recurrent one, thanks to the trauma she had unsuccessfully tried to help Neroli overcome.

Did Ocean View hospital even have security?

How far away were any police? The closest large town was Nelson and that would be at least ninety minutes away by road.

The tension escalated several more notches as the spokesmen for the gang members moved. His shoulders hunched and the fingers of one hand flexed and then clenched. The fist was thrust towards the only male member staff member present.

'Now!'

Just do what he says, Mike, Beth urged silently. *Please!* But Dr Harris hadn't even flinched.

'Sure.' Mike's face was impassive and Beth found herself suddenly feeling slightly more confident. Well into his fifties now, Ocean View hospital's emergency department consultant probably had more than enough experience to cope with situations such as this. 'But I'm not going to tolerate my staff—or anyone else—being intimidated.'

There was a tiny silence as each side weighed up the implications of non-cooperation. It was broken by a groan from the injured gang member and the attention of everybody present was instantly diverted.

'What's happened exactly?'

'He's been shot, man. I told you.'

'Yes, but where? And how long ago? How much blood has he lost?' Mike was moving calmly towards the victim. Beth looked at her nursing colleagues. Should they all follow him? Chelsea was looking as nervous as she felt herself, and Maureen looked grim. The older nurse tilted her head.

'Chelsea, why don't you and Beth go and get a stretcher? I'll stay and help Mike.' She turned as she spoke so that her back was towards the gang members. 'Call the police,' she whispered faintly, her lips barely moving. 'Fast.'

Chelsea's nervousness seemed to wear off the moment she was assigned a task. She even grinned at Beth as they hurried from the triage area.

'Here we go,' she said almost cheerfully. 'Again!'

Beth's heart sank to a new low. 'You mean you get this type of incident on a regular basis?'

'We do get bit of trouble from gangs now and then.' Chelsea paused as they entered the main section of the emergency department and she reached for the wall phone. 'You'd be used to it, though, wouldn't you? Didn't you say you've been working in south Auckland?'

'Yes, but I didn't expect…' Beth's words trailed off as Chelsea started speaking to whoever was on the other end of the phone.

'We seem to have a code yellow in ED,' she said briskly. She listened for only a few seconds. 'Cool…thanks.'

Beth grabbed the tail end of the stretcher and she and Chelsea headed back the moment the phone was replaced.

'What's a code yellow?'

'Trouble with gangs.'

Good grief! So it happened often enough to have its own code?

'What happens on a code yellow?'

'Sid will get here first. He's our night orderly cum security guard. Then one of the local cops who lives just down the road will come in.' Chelsea was looking almost excited now as she glanced back at Beth. 'If he thinks it's necessary, he'll call Nelson and they'll chopper in the armed offender squad to help out.'

'But there's only one patient!'

'So far.' Chelsea gave Beth a questioning glance now. 'This really bothers you, doesn't it?'

'I'm OK.' Beth wasn't about to demonstrate any inadequacy on her first shift. 'Like you said, I'm used to it. A bit too used to it, maybe. A friend of mine had a knife held to her throat by a gang member not so long ago.'

Chelsea looked horrified. 'Was she hurt?'

'Not physically. She's given up nursing, though, and gone to work in her sister's coffee-shop in Melbourne.'

'Was that why you decided to move as well?'

'Partly.' Beth smiled wryly as they turned the corner. 'I *was* rather hoping I'd be getting away from this kind of thing by moving down here.'

Chelsea's quick smile was sympathetic. 'I hope it wasn't the main incentive for the shift, then.'

'It wasn't.'

Beth's words were lost as they entered the front of the department to find the stretcher was now superfluous. The injured man's colleagues had dragged or lifted him as far as the bed in the empty resuscitation area.

'I said *don't* cut his leathers, man!'

'We've got to get his jacket off so I can assess his breathing.' Mike was still managing to sound calm but Beth could see that his frown lines had deepened perceptibly.

Maureen was plugging the tubing attached to an oxygen mask onto the overhead outlet. 'I'm just going to put this on your face,' she warned their patient.

The stream of obscene language made Maureen look even grimmer than she had on first spotting this patient.

'Airway appears clear,' she told Mike dryly. Stepping back as two silent gang members unceremoniously stripped the leather jacket off the now groaning man, she noticed the return of the younger nurses.

'Perhaps you two could clear Resus 2.' She and Mike seemed practised in trying to keep the atmosphere as casual as possible, but the undercurrent of urgency was easy enough for Beth to detect.

And no wonder. The man in the adjacent resuscitation area was looking alarmed and his wife was terrified. It was just as well that the chest pain he was having investigated had been deemed to be angina rather than a heart attack because otherwise the anxiety caused by the arrival of the new patient might have made his condition a lot worse. He probably didn't need admission but he certainly needed to be moved.

It took a minute or two to disentangle the patient from the ECG electrodes and other monitoring equipment anchoring him to the area. Beth looked over her shoulder as she pushed the foot end of the bed clear of Resus 2. The injured man in Resus 1 was alone with his medical attendants now. The other gang members had vanished. A second later they all heard the roar of an unmuffled engine as the car blocking the doors was restarted.

'Our first job is to clear the department of any other patients if it's possible,' Chelsea told Beth as they manoeuvred the bed along the corridor separating the emergency department from the rest of the hospital. 'We close the department to any arrivals that could be seen by a GP as well.' She shook her head. 'There was a major riot in the department a few years back apparently, and a bystander in the waiting room got stabbed. That was when code yellow came into force.'

Their patient's wife was clutching her handbag in both hands as she trotted beside the swiftly moving bed. 'Did you hear them say they were going to deal with whoever did the shooting? Where's it going to end?'

'At least most of them are out of the department for a while,' Chelsea responded. 'It'll give the police time to deal with them before there's any *real* trouble here.'

There was a curious calm in the emergency department when Beth and Chelsea returned. Mike was doing an ultrasound on the exposed, tattooed belly of their patient. Maureen was setting up a new bag of IV fluids.

A burly man wearing an orderly's uniform was standing with his arms folded by the head of the bed, and an equally solid man in police uniform stood in an identical pose at the foot. They both gave Beth a curious stare.

'Gidday,' the orderly said. 'You're new here, aren't you?'

'This is Beth,' Chelsea told them. 'It's her first shift tonight. Beth, this is Sid and that's Dennis.'

The nods and smiles from the two men were both welcoming and sympathetic. Not a great way to start a new job, they conveyed, but they were pleased to meet her and would make sure she was safe. And Beth smiled back. Suddenly things didn't seem nearly so disheartening. She would never have been introduced to members of security back-up in her old department and they certainly wouldn't have made any non-verbal promises about making sure she was looked after. Working in a small community *was* going to be different.

Better.

'Who's on call for surgery tonight?' Mike's query broke an almost companionable silence.

'Luke,' Maureen told him.

'Good. He won't mind being woken up.'

'Can you call him in, please, Chelsea?'

'Sure.'

Beth watched as Chelsea headed for the wall phone. She knew there were five surgeons associated with Ocean View hospital. Three general and two orthopaedic. What were the odds that one of them would end up being called Luke?

And how many other reminders would there be for her tonight to let her know that you could never really escape the past and make a brand-new start? Beth shook herself mentally, bending over to pick up packaging from dressings and IV gear that littered the floor.

For heaven's sake. It had been six years ago. It was pathetic that hearing that particular name could still have any effect on her. And it was weird that it was so much stronger tonight than it had been for a very long time. Maybe that was just because she was displaced. Feeling a little lost in a new environment and seeking links with her past to anchor herself.

'He's on his way,' Chelsea reported. 'Do you need theatre staff called in?'

Mike angled the ultrasound probe in a new direction, still peering at the screen. Then he nodded. 'Yes, thanks, Chels. I reckon Jackal here is going to need more of an inside look than I'm getting.'

The gang member's nickname suddenly seemed

quite appropriate. The flash of fear as the comprehension of what was being organised on his behalf filtered through was swiftly followed by an aggressive snarl.

'No way! You're not cutting me, man! I'm outta here.'

'*Oi!*' The barked response from both Sid and Dennis was not enough to stop Jackal making an unexpectedly vigorous move to sit up, ripping the IV line from his arm in the process and actually managing to swing both legs over the side of the bed.

Restrained by the larger men, who latched onto both arms, he subsided instantly. In fact, he looked decidedly green within seconds and then, much to Sid's obvious disgust, he vomited. Sid gamely kept hold of the arm but the restraint was no longer needed. Sitting up had been enough to cut an already diminished blood supply to Jackal's brain and his level of consciousness was dropping fast.

'Lay him down.' Mike sounded almost weary. 'And watch out for that blood, Sid.' The orderly was wearing gloves but Jackal's IV site was bleeding quite heavily. He leaned closer to their patient. 'Listen, mate. You're sick. You've had a bullet go through your belly. You're lucky it hasn't killed you but it's still done a lot of damage to your spleen. You're losing blood. Jump up now and you might make things a whole lot worse in a hurry.'

The response was not incoherent enough to disguise the obscenities but Mike simply straightened and reached for a fresh pair of gloves.

'I'll get that IV line back in. I don't think he's going to put up much of a fight with his blood pressure in his boots.'

Beth looked at the monitor. The pressure reading

was 85 over 40. Jackal had to be losing a significant amount of blood. The glance that passed between Sid and Dennis was significant. If this became a homicide, they could all be in for a lot more drama.

Maybe they would be anyway.

Beth handed Mike a new wide-bore cannula and was ready with the luer plug and flush moments later.

'Any word from Sally?'

'Sorry.' Beth shook her head. This was the kind of thing she hated about starting a new job. 'I don't know who Sally is.'

'She's one of our paramedics,' Maureen supplied. 'The ambulance got called not long after Jackal's mates took off from here.' Her brief smile was intended to be reassuring for Beth. 'Police back-up got activated at the same time.'

Beth nodded, pleased to find her hands steady as she completed the fiddly task of screwing the luer plug into place on the cannula hub. She was injecting a bolus of saline to check that the IV line was patent when the radio on the main desk crackled.

'Ambulance to ED. Do you copy?'

'Shall I get that?' Chelsea queried.

'I'll do it.' Mike stripped off his gloves and then glanced at Beth. 'Can you get some more fluids up?'

'Sure.'

Beth taped the cannula securely in place, having flushed the line. Then she reached for a giving set and a new bag of saline. The task was automatic enough not to distract her from listening to Mike as he reached for the microphone next to the radio set.

'Mike here, Sally. Receiving you loud and clear. What have you got?'

'Status one patient. Car vs pedestrian.'

'Roger.' Mike shook his head slowly as he pulled a pen from his shirt pocket. They all knew how unlikely this was to have been any accident. 'Vital signs?'

'Heart rate of 130. Respiration rate 36. Oxygen saturation down and blood pressure unrecordable at present. GCS of 8. Head and chest injuries. Multiple fractures.'

Sid and Dennis looked at each other again. They didn't need medical training to know that this patient was seriously unwell. Neither did they need the ambulance officer's confirmation that this was another code yellow patient.

The ETA of the ambulance was ten to fifteen minutes and any calm in the small emergency department vanished.

Extra staff began arriving as Beth and Chelsea were assigned the task of setting up Resus 2 in preparation for the new arrival.

'Have an intubation trolley ready,' Mike instructed. 'And a chest decompression kit.'

'What happens with serious chest injuries here?' Beth queried, pulling the crumpled sheet from the bed. 'We don't have a cardiothoracic surgeon, do we?'

Chelsea shook her head. 'We stabilise them and then chopper them to Wellington.' She flapped the clean sheet to spread it over the mattress. 'Same with head injuries. We don't run to a neurosurgeon either.'

Chelsea told Beth who the staff members were as the level of activity in the department steadily increased.

'That's Kelly—she's a radiographer. Seth is the house surgeon on call. Looks like Rowena's coming in to help as well. She's a midwife.'

The names flowed right over Beth's head. These people were all still strangers and this was no time to start even trying to remember names.

'And there's Luke.'

Beth flicked the laryngoscope she was checking shut to turn off its light. Despite herself, her head turned sharply at that familiar name but any view of the latest newcomer was blocked by the large figure of Dennis, the police officer.

'The ambulance is here,' he told them. 'I'm going to see if they need any help.'

Two other members of the local police force had accompanied the ambulance but the paramedics had been in no danger from the hit-and-run victim they were transporting.

'Breath sounds absent on the left side now.' A blonde woman had her stethoscope on the exposed chest, between ECG electrodes. 'GCS has been dropping steadily. I've already done a decompression on the right side.'

'Bring him straight in here.' Mike pointed to the available resuscitation area and Beth stepped back as the stretcher moved swiftly towards her. Then she reached to help transfer the patient to the bed.

'On the count of three,' Mike directed, holding the patient's head and neck still by supporting the cervical collar. 'One…two…three!'

'We think he was hit at a speed of at least sixty kilometres an hour,' the paramedic informed Mike. 'Apparently he was airborne for twenty to thirty metres.'

Maureen handed Beth a pair of shears. 'See what you can do to get rid of the clothing.'

Beth was aware of more people pressing into the resus area to assist.

'Tension pneumothorax on the left,' Mike confirmed tersely. 'Someone get me a decompression kit, please?'

'I can do that.'

The calm voice should have eased some of the tension but the shears in Beth's hands closed with an uncontrolled snap. Her gaze shifted just as emphatically to the speaker and for a split second she actually forgot what she was supposed to be doing.

Luke.

It couldn't be.

But it was.

Luke Savage.

At Ocean View hospital?

If Beth had tried to think of the last possible place on earth she would expect to see this man again, a small-town hospital would have been way up on the list. A prison cell might have beaten it to top spot, of course, but not by much.

He hadn't noticed her. The surgeon was completely focussed on the task of inserting a needle between the victim's ribs to release air trapped in his chest, which was preventing his lungs from functioning.

'Pelvis is unstable.' Mike was doing a survey for other major injuries while Luke was attempting to establish adequate breathing.

The consultant's statement was enough to start Beth's hands moving again, her momentary lapse unnoticed. She peeled leather trousers clear of the deformity on the right thigh.

'Open fracture of the femur,' she advised.

'Cover it,' Mike responded. 'We can't deal with that just yet.'

Beth reached for a large gauze dressing and tried to

concentrate on squeezing a sachet of saline onto the pad to dampen it, but she simply couldn't help glancing back towards Luke.

Had Luke recognised her voice as easily as she had recognised his?

Apparently not.

'Oxygen sats aren't climbing.' Luke was staring at the monitor above the bed. 'We'll have to intubate.'

'I'll get another IV line going,' Mike said. 'We need to speed up this fluid resus.'

A new face peered in through the curtain. 'Luke? They just called to say they're ready for you in Theatre.'

His glance seemed to bypass Beth effortlessly as she used the damp dressing to cover the gaping wound on their patient's leg. 'Thanks. I'll be up as soon as I can.'

Mike took the cannula Beth was holding out for him. 'Could you help Sid take Jackal upstairs, please?'

'Sure.' The prospect of making an exit was appealing.

Was Luke simply being professional, ignoring her— quite properly—due to the emergency treatment of a patient? It was possible that he had not yet recognised or even noticed her.

It was also quite possible that he just didn't give a damn.

And why, in God's name, should that bother her so much anyway?

Beth turned her back on Luke but she wasn't going to escape quite so easily. The sound of breaking glass made everybody pause.

'What the hell was that?'

'We locked the doors when we came in.' The male ambulance officer had abandoned his paperwork to step closer. 'Sounds like someone really wants to get in.'

A police officer appeared behind him. 'ETA for the

chopper is only two minutes. We've got a bit of a skirmish going on in the car park right now, though.'

The sound of a shotgun being fired was unmistakable.

So was the alarm that sounded on the new patient's monitor in the tiny silence that followed.

'He's in VF,' Luke warned.

Mike was already reaching for the defibrillator paddles. 'Everyone stand clear.'

'I don't want anyone moving from here until we get some back-up,' the police officer ordered.

'Stand clear,' Mike ordered.

Beth stood clear. In fact, she was quickly penned into the corner of the area, along with the paramedic and Chelsea, and couldn't escape the awareness of how appalling the situation was.

They watched as Maureen squeezed air into the patient's lungs and Luke readied himself to do compressions when the initial series of shocks was completed. Mike pressed the paddles into position and pressed the buttons to deliver the second shock and then the third.

Beth closed her eyes for a moment. This was all so bizarre it was almost a joke. Some huge, cosmic joke. And whoever decided which way the winds of fate were going to blow was laughing at her right now.

She had come here to get away from the stress of dealing with violence and was now up to her neck in the most major incident she had ever encountered.

And she had also come to get away from the lingering effect Luke Savage had branded on her life. She had just ended her extremely brief engagement to Brent, for heaven's sake, because she had recognised that the only qualities he had that were attractive had been the ones that reminded her of Luke.

The prospect of actually crossing paths with Luke
Savage had haunted Beth for far longer than the fear of
finding herself living Neroli's nightmare, and coming
to a small town like Hereford had seemed like the perfect way to escape that particular ghost.

And here she was, only a few feet away from the
man. And it felt like the first time she had seen him all
over again. He was just as physically attractive, but it
hadn't been simply his looks that had drawn her so con-
vincingly at that first meeting. It had been his presence.
The feeling she'd got that this man would be able to handle any situation he found himself in, no matter what it
was. And she could feel that again right now. Luke was
just…exactly the same.

It was so bizarre. It went way beyond being a disappointing start to a new beginning. This was gutting.
Maybe she *should* have taken up Neroli's invitation to
go to Australia with her. Melbourne would be a nice
place to live and Neroli's sister was always short of
waitresses in that coffee-shop.

The static cleared from the monitor screen after the
third shock to show a pattern that settled over several
seconds into normal sinus rhythm. The quiet was broken by the steadying beeps of the monitor, loud but
muffled shouting from somewhere outside and then the
crescendo of an approaching helicopter's rotors.

Relieved glances were exchanged between staff
members and it was only then that Beth's gaze met that
of Luke. The, oh, so familiar dark grey eyes beneath
that shaggy mop of black hair widened and Beth realised that he hadn't been ignoring her.

He couldn't look this shocked if he had known she
was so close.

Her presence was a surprise. And it wasn't a pleasant one.

It shouldn't have hurt but it did. Any fantasies she'd ever had of looking into those eyes again and seeing the love that had once been there were crushed in an instant, and Beth could hear echoes of that cosmic laughter.

She wanted nothing more than to get away, and Mike's repeated instruction to help shift Jackal up to Theatre seemed timely.

It wasn't until Beth pulled the curtain back and stepped outside the resuscitation area that they realised the move had been premature.

Black-clad, helmeted and armed offender squad members were filing rapidly into the emergency department of Ocean View hospital, but the skirmish that had been taking place outside had also moved in. Somehow one of Jackal's mates had gained access and was now standing outside Resus 1 with a knife in his hand as a member of an obviously rival gang advanced rapidly towards him.

And Beth had inadvertently stepped right between them.

Was this the punchline of the joke?

There was nobody close enough to help but the fear that should have swamped and immobilised Beth simply wasn't there.

'Don't even *think* about it!' she snapped.

Beth drew herself up to her full height of a not very impressive five feet four inches. Her lack of height was irrelevant because the misery over the personal disaster she had engineered for herself in coming here had just morphed into pure fury.

'You!' She jabbed her finger at the leather-clad chest of the man whose progress towards Resus 1 she had just blocked. He was at least six feet tall and his bearded, tattooed face was bleeding heavily from a jagged laceration. 'Go and *sit* down and behave yourself.'

Whirling to confront Jackal's mate, Beth was dimly aware that the police officers rushing to her assistance had slowed involuntarily, their jaws drooping.

'Drop the knife,' she commanded.

'*No!*' she yelled as both men made a move to close her further into the middle of the potentially very dangerous human sandwich. Her voice remained at a furious shout. 'Do as you're bloody well *told*! I am just *so* not in the mood for this.'

Amazingly, the gang members froze. The hand holding the lethal-looking knife began to drop and suddenly the police were right there. As fast as the incident had occurred, it was defused and the space cleared.

Beth was aware of a curious shaking sensation in her knees. She turned her head slowly to see the occupants of Resus 2 staring at her.

'Woo-hoo!' Chelsea called softly. 'You go, girl!'

Mike had an astonished grin on his face but it was Luke who drew Beth's gaze. He was staring at her as well, of course. Who wouldn't be? He wasn't looking shocked any more. He was looking as though Beth were a complete stranger.

A rather impressive stranger, in fact.

Straightening her back made that weak-kneed sensation subside almost completely. The calm, confident smile Beth was aiming for probably came out more like an embarrassed grin, but it didn't seem to dull the respect she could detect from her small audience.

An audience that included Luke Savage.

How cool was that?

CHAPTER TWO

GOOD grief!

Luke was still shaking his head in disbelief as he scrubbed up for Jackal's emergency laparotomy ten minutes later.

Seeing Beth again after all these years was unbelievable enough. Seeing her doing that warrior princess act with the gang members had been…

The sexiest damn thing Luke had ever seen in his life.

He scrubbed beneath his nails hard enough to cause real pain.

Beth was the only woman who had ever made him seriously consider marriage.

And she was the only woman who had ever dumped him.

The hurt and the ensuing anger that had caused should have been rendered inconsequential by the blows life had meted out since then, so it was incredibly disturbing to find how easily the years could be peeled back.

One good look into those bright blue eyes and there he was again. Not measuring up. Just not being good enough, no matter how much love he had to offer.

What the hell was Beth doing in Hereford of all places?

Luke took his foot off the water control and reached for a sterile towel. She'd probably come here to give her kids a nice, healthy rural upbringing or something. Snapping on gloves, Luke turned abruptly to let the scrub nurse tie up his gown. That flash of something astonishingly like jealousy at the thought of the father of those children was ridiculous.

So she was still an attractive woman. So what?

So she had grown up a bit and become brave about confronting things she didn't like. Again, so what?

Luke had more than enough to deal with in his life right now, without complicating things by renewing any kind of relationship with Beth. The last thing he needed was to try poking an old scarred area when the potential to find a tender spot was so clearly possible.

A deep breath was called for here. And rational thinking. This disturbance was probably just part of the surprise factor of seeing Beth again. All he needed to do was ride it through and there would be no shortage of distractions if that proved in any way difficult. It was a relief to use the one immediately available.

'Let's get this show on the road, shall we?'

With his hands held carefully crossed in front of his chest, Luke used his shoulder to push open the swing doors into Theatre.

At just after 3 a.m. on a Tuesday morning, Ocean View's emergency department was stretched to slightly over its full capacity.

One of the high-tech resuscitation areas was still occupied by a seriously injured patient, the other one having just been vacated by the hit-and-run victim, who had gone up to Theatre 2 for the attention of an orthopaedic surgeon. All the beds in the cubicled area were also full and half of those patients were still waiting to have bones X-rayed or lacerations sutured. The treatment rooms were full and there were no spare seats in the waiting area either.

A few people with minor injuries were in Reception but most of them were simply there to offer solidarity to their mates, and they included some of the loudest and most unpleasant women Beth had ever encountered.

They were all unkempt, tattooed, pierced in multiple places and inebriated, and only too happy to demonstrate their contempt of any authority figures or lack of appreciation for any medical assistance. But the police presence was strong enough to ensure the safety of staff and the background noise of obscene language and shouting was so constant Beth could tune it out now.

It had already become automatic to seek the company of a police officer before approaching or treating a patient, and all the nurses remembered to wait until a member of one gang had left the X-ray department before escorting a member from the rival gang down the corridor.

Hopefully, the stab victim who was currently in Resus 1 would also be sent up to Theatre soon. When the doctors could be freed from attending the critically injured patients they should be able to deal with the minor injuries rapidly. They would be able to clear the department and then they could all have a well-deserved break.

Oddly enough, the chaos and unpleasantness of her current environment had been quite enjoyable over the last hour or so. Not the patients, of course, but their uniform lack of co-operation or appreciation had provided a bond of camaraderie amongst the staff members that had only increased under pressure.

And Beth was very firmly one of them. Thanks to that inadvertent episode of venting her tension, having stepped into the path of the converging gang members, Beth had not only been welcomed into the ranks of Ocean View's emergency department staff, she was currently being used as a lynchpin.

Even though it had only taken a few seconds and could quite easily have been a huge mistake, the fact that Beth had taken control had become a kind of emotional bank in which snippets of humour or stamina were being deposited and could be withdrawn whenever someone needed the lift of a shared smile or a pat on the back.

'I'm just *so* not in the mood for this' had become the catch-phrase of the night and never failed to produce a smile.

Dennis, the local cop, had claimed Beth as one of their own with a hint of pride.

'Keep your eyes open,' he had told one of the Nelson police officers about to accompany Beth when she needed an escort to Radiology. 'You might learn something from our Beth they never thought to teach you at police college.'

How ironic that Beth could feel so at home in a new place so quickly when she was still having serious doubts about the wisdom of having come here at all. She even knew her way around the storeroom now, having gone in there so often to fetch new supplies, and she was there again now, checking the fridge, as requested, to see how much O-negative blood they had on hand. Then she moved towards the shelves supporting boxes of dressings.

A number of extra-large gauze pads had been needed

to staunch the arterial flow from the blood vessel severed by a knife wound in the car-park skirmish. And a fresh intubation pack was needed to restock Resus 2. Searching for the location of cuffed endotracheal tubes, Beth's eye was caught by the sterilised, draped rolls of surgical gear.

The obstetric pack was probably useful, but how often would they have the need for a thoracotomy kit here? Beth had only ever seen someone's chest opened in an emergency department once, and that had only been done because it had been in a big hospital and they'd had a cardiothoracic surgeon available for back-up.

Luke had had ambitions in cardiothoracic surgery so why on earth was he working here? And how could Beth hope to start a new life when there would be such constant reminders of the past?

If she didn't stay at Ocean View, though, would she end up being back in some emergency department large enough for the triage staff to wear headsets and microphones? Beth's sigh was heartfelt. She had really been looking forward to the change of working in a much smaller and potentially friendlier environment. And what on earth was she going to say to the nurse manager?

Sorry. This is a great place to work but I can't possibly stay because the man I was passionately in love with years ago happens to be working here as well, and I'm not sure if I could handle seeing him every day.

How pathetic was that?

Especially when it had been her that had broken up the relationship.

Beth added some other sizes of gauze dressings to the load she was carrying and wondered how the supplies

of lignocaine were holding up. A lot of local anaesthetic was being used in the repair of lacerations. The
thought was only fleeting, however, and Beth did not
reach for any ampoules. She was too busy thinking
about something else.

It hadn't *been* her that had broken things up, though,
had it? Not really. Ending it had been the last thing Beth
had wanted. And having her nose rubbed in the puddle
of her lost dreams by living in the same small town as
Luke Savage was just unthinkable.

And finding him beside the bed of the stabbing victim in Resus 1 was unexpected enough to add considerably to those doubts about her new job. She had
thought Luke would be tied up in Theatre for the rest of
the night and that maybe encounters with the surgeon
would be the exception rather than the rule. Beth averted
her gaze hurriedly to avoid renewed eye contact but the
surgeon was listening too intently to Mike to notice the
arrival of a nurse carrying supplies.

'...femoral artery,' Mike was saying. 'Class III haem-
orrhage. Estimated blood loss of around two litres, but
we've finally got it under control with the pressure
bandage.'

'Blood pressure?'

'Coming up finally. Ninety-five on fifty now. We've
run in two litres of saline and I'm just waiting for blood
results.'

Beth was behind Luke now. It was quite safe to risk
a glance. Not that she needed to confirm the impressions
gained earlier, but it was tempting to add to them.

The shaggy black hair was a little longer than it used
to be and there was just a hint of silver at his temples.
Thirty-six seemed a bit young to be going grey, but

Beth had found the odd white hair amongst her own recently and she was two years younger than Luke.

His face was browner and leaner, which made him look more serious somehow. Judging by the arms and the smooth V of chest visible around the baggy scrub suit, the rest of Luke's body was browner and leaner than it used to be as well.

Beth had to take a rather deep breath all of a sudden. No. Luke Savage had not lost his looks in the last ten years. Quite the reverse, really…damn it!

'Beth?'

'Sorry, were you talking to me?'

'I just wondered how the supplies of O-neg were looking.'

'There's two units. Plus some packed cells.' Beth continued putting the dressings into the drawer of the trolley but it would have been rude not to look up again. Mike was nodding. Luke was looking at the patient.

'How are you feeling?' he queried.

The gang member gave a noncommittal grunt.

'We're going to have to take you up to Theatre and repair that gash in your leg,' Luke explained. 'Have you had anything to eat or drink in the last four hours?'

'Yeah. I had a feed.'

'How long ago was that?'

'Dunno.'

'And you've been drinking?' The question was superfluous, given the smell of alcohol that hung over most of their patients that night, but Luke managed to sound nonjudgmental.

'Yeah. Had a few beers, man.'

The gang member actually smiled at Luke. 'You going to fix up my leg, then?'

Beth was slipping out of the cubicle as Luke turned towards Mike. 'Looks stable enough to go upstairs. We should be ready in twenty minutes or so, I guess. What about…?'

Beth was now far enough away for Luke's voice to be covered by the general noise in the department. Or maybe it was because the noise level had suddenly increased out here. A wave of weariness hit as Beth wondered if she needed to call for more police assistance.

But it was a police officer who was doing the calling.

'Help! We need some help here.'

Beth moved fast towards the reception area. She could see a woman lying on the floor near the seats in the waiting room. Another woman was struggling to get away from the grip the police officer had on her arm.

'I *told* you Stella was sick,' the woman shouted. 'And you wouldn't listen, you bastard!' She kicked at the officer, who winced but held on.

Beth dropped to a crouch, reaching to shake the apparently unconscious woman's shoulder.

'Stella? Can you hear me?' With no response to the shaking, Beth pinched the woman's ear lobe. 'Open your eyes.'

The woman groaned and rolled her head from side to side. Beth could see her chest rising and the groans were loud enough to suggest that her airway was clear. She was feeling for a pulse on the woman's wrist as she heard a deep voice behind her.

'What's happened?'

'She fainted or something,' the police officer said. 'One minute she was sitting on that chair and the next she was on the floor.'

'She's been bloody *hurt*, that's why!' The second

woman was clearly furious. 'She's been feeling like crap but nobody would *listen*!' With the stream of ob-scenities that followed this statement, it didn't surprise Beth that nobody had wanted to listen. Still, there was no excuse for missing a potentially serious injury.

Luke was frowning as though he'd had the same thought. He crouched down close to Beth and put his fingers on the woman's neck, feeling for a carotid pulse.

'There's no radial pulse,' Beth told him quietly.

Luke nodded, acknowledging the information that the woman's blood pressure had to be very low. He glanced up at the people standing nearby. 'Can some-body tell us what happened to her?'

'She got hit in the chest,' the second woman spat. 'With a bloody softball bat, that's what *happened*.'

'How long ago?'

But Luke's query was ignored.

'And it was that bitch over there that did it. And I'm going to *do* something about it.'

Fortunately, two more police officers arrived to deal with the woman who was making a new and more fren-zied attempt to get free.

'It must have happened in the car park,' the first of-ficer told Luke. 'Probably well over an hour ago.'

'Thanks.' Luke slid an arm beneath the woman's back, the other under her legs, standing up with appar-ent ease despite the weight of his burden. 'Let's go,' he said to Beth. 'What's free?'

'Resus 2.' Beth led the way, relieved to move away from the tension in the waiting area, which was now es-calating thanks to the screams of their new patient's friend.

'Let me *go*! Where are you taking her? She's bloody *dead*, isn't she?'

Stella wasn't dead but she wasn't looking at all well. Mike came into Resus 2 as Luke gently deposited the woman on the bed.

'What's happened?'

'Collapse,' Luke told him succinctly. 'Possible blunt chest trauma from a softball bat more than an hour ago.'

Beth slipped an oxygen mask over the woman's face and turned the flow up to 10 litres a minute, before swiftly turning her attention to pulling open Stella's shirt. Then she grabbed a pair of shears to cut through the singlet top beneath the shirt.

'She's tachycardic,' Luke told his colleague. 'And she's got JVD.'

Beth hadn't noticed the distension of the jugular veins on the woman's neck but she recognised the significance of the sign, reaching for the ECG leads as she dropped the shears.

'Chest-wall contusion,' she reported.

Stella groaned loudly, swore incoherently and tried to move as Mike put his hands on the obviously bruised area on the left side of her chest.

'It's all right,' he reassured their patient. 'We're just checking you out.' He looked up. 'Do we know her name?'

'Stella,' Beth supplied.

'I know it hurts, Stella. Hang in there.' He looked up again. 'Fractured ribs,' he said. 'But she seems to be moving air all right.'

Luke had wrapped a BP cuff just below the tattoo encircling Stella's upper arm. 'Hypotensive,' he noted. 'Systolic's barely 80. Let's get an IV started.'

'Make it two,' Mike said. 'Beth, can you get a line in on your side, please?'

'Sure.' Beth stuck the last ECG electrode in place and

turned to grab a tourniquet. Mike was watching the screen of the cardiac monitor.

'Sinus tachycardia,' he said. 'And…yes, we've got electrical alternans.'

Luke's grunt sounded almost satisfied as he pulled the cap off a cannula. 'Thought so. Pericardial tamponade.'

Beth glanced up at the screen, noting the way the spikes of the QRS changed direction every few beats, indicating a change in the cardiac axis. She knew the first line of treatment for an acute pericardial tamponade was a rapid infusion of saline. Bleeding around the heart, trapped by the membrane encasing the organ, was interfering with its ability to pump blood. By increasing the fluid volume of the patient, the output of the heart could be improved.

Pleased to have known to choose a wide-bore cannula without being told, Beth had also gone for easy venous access inside the left elbow. The cannula slid into place and she occluded the vein at the end of the tubing as she withdrew the needle and reached for a luer plug.

Luke was reaching for a luer plug as well. For a split second they caught each other's gaze and there was a hint of a smile lurking on the surgeon's face.

'Snap,' he murmured. 'Guess we'll have to call that one a draw.'

Mike watched them both as they finished attaching giving sets and started the fluids running. 'Definitely a draw.' He smiled. 'Nice work.' Then his face settled into a frown of concentration as he placed his stethoscope on Stella's chest.

'Heart sounds are pretty muffled.'

'Jugular veins are more distended now.'

'Stella!' Mike raised his voice. 'Open your eyes for me.'

There was no response. Mike pinched her ear lobe but her level of consciousness had dropped enough for the pain to be ignored. 'GCS is dropping,' he warned.

'Beck's triad.'

Beth wasn't aware she spoken aloud until she caught Mike's glance. 'You know your stuff, don't you?' The older consultant sounded impressed. 'What do we do next, then?'

'Pericardiocentesis?' Beth *was* aware that Luke was watching her. She'd been little more than a student nurse when they had worked together all those years ago. Would he also be impressed at the level of knowledge and the skills she had acquired since then? 'Removal of as little as 20 mils of blood can improve cardiac output and patient condition considerably, can't it?'

'Spot on.' Mike nodded. 'You'll find the kit on the shelf above the IV cannulas.'

Luke drew up the local anaesthetic while Beth swabbed the skin on Stella's chest. Mike inserted the six-inch, plastic-sheathed needle, aiming towards the base of the heart, and they all watched the monitor screen carefully for ECG changes.

'QRS complex is widening,' Luke warned at one point. 'Draw back a little, Mike.'

Beth held her breath. If it wasn't blood around Stella's heart that was causing the problem then their patient was in serious trouble. She relaxed slightly as she saw the needle fill with blood.

'Here we go.' Mike drew back on the syringe. 'Five mils,' he noted. 'Ten...fifteen...'

Then the flow stopped. It seemed that enough blood should have been removed to help, but there was no improvement in Stella's condition. In fact, it got worse.

The ECG began to change, with the heart speeding up and missing beats. Stella wasn't moving or even groaning any longer.

And then Chelsea called out from the adjoining resuscitation area.

'Mike? He's bleeding again. I can't seem to find the right spot to apply manual pressure. Shall I take the bandage off?'

'Coming.' Mike glanced up at Luke. 'Can you manage?'

Luke glanced at Beth. 'Sure.'

The management of the femoral artery bleed next door was obviously difficult and the rest of the department was still humming. Nobody could be spared to assist in Resus 2 even when Stella's heart gave up the struggle of trying to pump against constriction.

The electrical stimulus was still there but their patient was pulseless and Luke's attempt to draw more blood from the pericardium with the needle proved fruitless.

'Start CPR,' he instructed Beth.

She worked hard to make her chest compressions as effective as possible, but Luke shook his head as he felt for a carotid pulse moments later.

'We're still not getting a pulse.' He raised his voice. 'Mike? I'm going to have to go for a thoracotomy here.'

Beth's jaw dropped but Mike sounded perfectly calm. 'That's fine,' he called back. 'I'll come and intubate for you in a second.'

Luke had caught Beth's astonished expression and his tone suggested he had taken her reaction as a personal criticism. 'You'll find a thoracotomy kit in the storeroom, Beth.'

She was pleased to be able to turn away. 'I know where it is.'

He *was* a surgeon after all, and maybe Luke had had experience with opening people's chests. He certainly seemed confident enough, and it was probably the only procedure that was going to save a life here, but it was still horrific to watch him divide Stella's sternum with a saw in what seemed like only a few minutes later.

It was just as well she'd had theatre experience in the past, Beth decided, handing instruments and wound towels to Luke. It was how they'd met in the first place. Luke had been a surgical registrar and Beth had just been starting work as a theatre nurse. She'd transferred, of course, when their relationship had hit the rocks and the fascination and pressure of working in the emergency department had gone from being a welcome distraction to a real passion.

And here they were again. The bizarre impression of being in a time warp was heightened after Luke took a scalpel and carefully incised the membrane of the pericardium. The rush of blood wasn't enough to suggest a fatal cardiac injury and there was a collective sigh of relief as the vigorous pumping of Stella's heart could be actually seen.

Mike had his fingers on the side of Stella's neck. 'Great output,' he said delightedly. 'Fantastic!'

His voice startled Beth. The feeling that she and Luke had been a single—and isolated—unit had been so strong she had actually forgotten Mike was there in the last few minutes. She had been standing so close to Luke. Their hands had touched more than once when she had handed him instruments, and that closeness—that touch—had wrapped them into a space that had been theirs alone.

Luke merely nodded in response to Mike's delight. 'We're not out of the woods quite yet,' he warned. 'Let's cover everything with dressings and sterile drapes and get her up to Theatre to finish.'

But he paused fractionally when he caught Beth's gaze and for the third time that night she was trapped by the expression in those dark grey eyes.

There was no hint of displeasure in them this time. Or the suggestion that she had changed beyond recognition. And, very oddly, the flicker of warmth that she saw was far more of a shock than Luke's earlier reactions to seeing her had been.

His voice touched exactly the same tender place as that fleeting glance had.

'Thanks, Beth,' Luke said softly. 'You were *brilliant*.'

CHAPTER THREE

IT WOULDN'T go away.

That flash of warmth in Luke's gaze had been contagious, and Beth could still feel it, hours later, when she was finally able to follow Chelsea to the staffroom where Maureen was making a pot of tea.

She could still abandon her new job and leave Hereford, she reminded herself as she sank gratefully onto a chair. Her head was telling her that in no uncertain terms again and again. Her heart, on the other hand, was insufferably smug in the knowledge of how difficult it would be her to talk herself into walking away. From this place. From the new job.

From Luke Savage.

And all it had taken had been that one little spark from the warmth in those grey eyes and the tone of his voice when he'd said she'd been brilliant.

Brilliant!

Beth's toes actually curled inside her shoes as a new wash of the glow spread through her.

'You're looking happy.' Maureen placed a steaming mug on the table in front of Beth. 'Sugar?'

'No, thanks.'

'I reckon she's just relieved it's all over.' Chelsea reached for the sugar bowl. 'What a night!'

Beth smiled wryly. 'It'll certainly go down in history as the most memorable first shift I've ever had at work, that's for sure.'

And the major incident with the gang members had only been the half of it.

'You did an amazing job out there.' Maureen pushed a plate of chocolate biscuits closer to Beth. 'Well done.'

'Yeah…' Chelsea was eyeing Beth curiously. 'You were brilliant.'

Beth hadn't blushed like that since she'd been a teenager. She reached for a biscuit to cover an embarrassment that had little to do with any modesty concerning her professional skills.

It hadn't been the first time she had been a key player in a dramatic life-and-death scenario in an emergency department. Not that she'd assisted with a thoracotomy, of course—in a big department there was always a queue of more senior staff eager to participate in something that big, but there had been that emergency Caesarean that time. And the puncture wound in a carotid artery and…

And none of that history mattered a damn because any praise that had come her way had been strictly professional.

As the comment that Chelsea appeared to have overheard from Luke had been, she reminded herself firmly.

But it hadn't *felt* like that, had it? The approbation from Luke had touched a place that hadn't been touched since…since…

Since she had been Luke's lover.

Beth crushed the thought relentlessly because

Chelsea was still giving her an odd look. As though she was determined to read her mind.

So was Maureen, come to that. Beth's eyebrows rose sharply.

'What?' she asked. 'Have I got chocolate all over my nose or something?'

'We're just curious,' Maureen explained.

'About the thoracotomy?'

Chelsea laughed. 'No. About whether you're going to ask or not.'

Beth was mystified. 'Ask what?'

'What every new female staff member always asks.'

So the interest had to concern a male staff member, and Beth suddenly knew exactly whom Chelsea had in mind. She could stop this conversation right now. Change the subject. Pretend that an urgent trip to the bathroom was called for. But her mouth had other ideas. It smiled.

'Which is?'

Chelsea exchanged another significant glance with Maureen. 'Whether Luke Savage is married or not, of course.'

The fact that the answer was expected did not stop Beth's heart stumbling over the next beat or two, but she actually laughed and shook her head in a valiant attempt to feign indifference. She picked up her mug of tea with a remarkably steady hand and took a sip.

Her lack of any verbal response did not faze Chelsea but she did seem puzzled.

'Well, that's a first, then.'

'What? A woman not throwing herself at Luke Savage?'

'Yep.'

Beth couldn't pretend to be all that surprised. She'd had a vivid reminder tonight of what it had been like the first time *she* had clapped eyes on Luke. There must be countless women out there who would feel that same level of attraction. What was surprising was the distinct impression she was getting that Luke was, in fact, still single.

'Not that any of them succeed,' Chelsea added wistfully enough for Beth to wonder if she had been one of those women herself. 'Maureen and I have a kind of running bet to guess how long it will take for them to realise he's not interested.'

That explained the significant glances but it left rather a lot still not explained.

Like *why* was Luke not interested in the women who clearly made themselves easily available?

Why was he *here*? In a medical backwater that lacked so much of the resources a larger hospital would have in the way of specialty expertise and facilities?

And *why* was she experiencing such an overwhelming level of curiosity?

The need to escape took on greater urgency and Beth glanced up at the wall clock.

'Nearly time to go home,' she said in relief. 'Is there anything I should be doing before the day shift arrives?'

'No.' Maureen smiled at Beth. 'You go and get some sleep. You've done more than enough on your first shift. We'll take care of the paperwork and handover.' She waved aside the protest Beth was clearly about to make. 'Go on,' she ordered. 'And if you see Mike out there, tell him his cup of tea's getting cold. I don't know why he hasn't come in yet.'

* * *

Beth soon found out. Mike was leaning against the central desk, in a now deserted department, talking to Luke. Both men looked exhausted but Beth could sense their satisfaction.

'How's Stella?' she queried.

'Stable,' Luke answered. 'We'll be transferring her to Wellington pretty soon.'

'Thanks to you two,' Mike added. 'You're a pretty good team, aren't you?'

Beth gritted her teeth. The old wound must have opened more than she had realised for Mike's words to have the effect of rubbing salt into it. This wasn't good.

'Runs in the blood for Beth, mind you,' Luke told Mike lightly. 'Did you know that her father is Nigel Dawson?'

Beth could barely suppress her groan. Of course Mike didn't know. It was the last thing *she'd* be pointing out to any new colleagues.

'Not the Nigel Dawson of heart-transplant fame?'

'That's the one.'

Mike's glance towards Beth was openly interested but it was Luke he directed his comment to. 'How on earth did you know that?'

'Beth and I worked together for a while, years ago.' Luke made it sound completely impersonal. 'She did a stint as a theatre nurse.'

'Lucky for Stella that you did.' Mike was smiling warmly at Beth but it was almost impossible to return the gesture.

Not only had Luke dismissed their past relationship as not rating a mention, he had revealed a large chunk of Beth's personal history that had been the other major part of her past she had been hoping to leave behind in coming to Hereford. It was the last straw and the balance finally tipped. No. Thanks to Luke, there was no way she could envisage the future she'd hoped to find here.

'I'd better go,' she said aloud.

Of course, her new colleagues couldn't detect any undertones to her statement. They both smiled understandingly.

'I'll walk you out to your car,' Luke offered.

'No need, thanks. I'm walking.'

'I'll come anyway,' Luke said infuriatingly. 'I need to grab my shaving gear from my car. Besides, we haven't even said hello properly, Beth.'

Beth ignored the quirk of Mike's eyebrow but she could feel her shoulders slump as she turned away. On top of discussing her famous father, she could just imagine how interested Chelsea and Maureen would be to hear that Luke was insisting on escorting her out of the building.

Her first shift at Ocean View hospital was ending with just as much of a disaster as it had begun with. Beth was in no mood to give a polite response to Luke's query about how she was.

'I would have been a lot better if you hadn't told Mike who my father was.'

Luke looked justifiably taken aback by her sharp tone. 'What's the problem? He *is* your father.'

Beth couldn't deny it, however much she would have preferred to. 'I came to Hereford to make a new start,' she said curtly. 'My family was one of the things I was more than happy to leave behind. Now I'm going to have everybody I meet asking questions.'

The calm, early morning sunshine that they emerged

into made the drama of the last six hours seem totally
unreal. This conversation with Luke seemed just as unreal. How crazy that they could slip back into an argu-
ment the first time they got to talk to each other.

'Well, I'm sorry.' Luke didn't sound sorry at all. 'But
what's so wrong with your family? If he was my father
I'd be proud of what he's achieved in his career.'

'Yeah...*you* would.'

'What's that supposed to mean?'

The tone was enough to force Beth to slow her pace
and turn to face Luke. He looked so tired, she thought.
And annoyed. And genuinely puzzled.

'Your opinion of my father was always higher than
mine.'

'I only met the man once. If you remember, you kept
me away from your family for so long I thought you
were an orphan.' Luke shook his head. 'For heaven's
sake, Beth. When did you start hating your father?'

'I don't hate him. I don't hate any of my family.
They're strangers.' Beth's anger was more than ready to
spill out. Gone were the days when she had responded
to a conflict by bottling things up. 'We were just an item
to add to our parents' CVs. Our son, the cardiologist.
Our daughter, the paediatrician. Oh, there's Beth, of
course, but the only thing she ever did that we really approved of was to produce Luke Savage as a potential
son-in-law.'

Luke had stopped walking completely now. He was
staring at Beth with that look she had seen earlier. The
one that implied she was a total stranger.

He opened his mouth but Beth didn't give him a
chance to say anything.

'I wanted to escape from that "not living up to the

family tradition" rubbish. Now, thanks to you, that's going to be impossible.'

Luke merely blinked. 'Was that all you came to Hereford to escape from?'

'What?'

'Is there anything else I should know about so I don't put my foot in my mouth and make your new start any more difficult for you?' Luke didn't actually sound as though he was trying to be helpful. His polite tone had a distinct edge of sarcasm. 'Have you left a boyfriend behind as well perhaps? Or a husband maybe?'

The tone pushed a button Beth had almost forgotten about. As if he cared about any answer she might supply!

'A fiancé, actually.'

The effect on Luke was quite satisfying. His jaw dropped. 'You're *engaged*?'

'Not any more.'

Luke's expression became carefully blank, as though a switch had been thrown. 'Who finished it?' he asked quietly. 'You…or him?'

'Me.' Beth glared at Luke. Just how much of her past was going to be dragged up before she could even find some time alone to come to terms with it all? It had gone beyond any kind of joke, however unfunny. Right now, it felt like her entire life was unravelling.

Luke met Beth's glare without moving a muscle. 'Not good enough for you, huh?' he suggested casually.

Beth could feel the heat leaving her gaze but she couldn't drag her eyes away from Luke. What would he say if he knew that her fiancé hadn't measured up because it was Luke who had set the standard? Staying in a relationship with Brent would have been settling for second best. No, not even that close. It would have been stepping onto another emotional planet.

The thought was gone as quickly as it had come and Beth could feel her anger draining, but it was Luke who looked away first.

'Maybe I should start a club,' he muttered. He turned towards a black Jeep parked nearby. He took a step away from Beth then stopped again. Luke looked more than tired now. He looked…sad.

'You've changed, Beth. I would never have thought you could stand up to trouble with gang members like that. Or start hating your family. Or go around dumping fiancés. I don't feel like I even know you any more.'

The sadness in Luke's expression was enough to bring the sting of tears to Beth's eyes and she turned away quickly to hide them.

'You never did, Luke,' she said softly. 'That was the problem, wasn't it?'

The walk to the motel unit the hospital was providing until she found somewhere to live was not long enough to calm the spin-cycle effect Beth's brain was having on her thoughts, and despite her exhaustion she knew she had no hope of sleeping yet. A walk on the deserted beach over the road from the motel seemed the perfect way to wait out the cycle.

Somewhere beneath the emotional roller-coaster the night had provided was a quiet pride in the fact that she had actually coped with it all. And the knowledge that she could cope again, if she had to. She wasn't going to follow Neroli's path and give up the work she loved because of intimidating patients.

Seeing Luke again had been just as much of a shock.

But she had coped with that, too. Or had she? Somehow, it was crushingly disappointing that their conversation in the car park had ended up feeling just like one of the arguments that had marked the disintegration of their relationship. Nothing had changed.

But everything had changed. There was something different about Luke. A mystery that was never going to be solved if Beth didn't stay in Hereford long enough to find out why Luke had chosen this quiet place to live and work.

And the tension created in the car park was never going to be resolved the way the old arguments had been. Until that last, horrible conflict, they had always made up their differences...in bed.

Any lingering tension would have been channelled into love-making that had made anything else totally insignificant. The world could have stopped turning as far as Beth was concerned when she had been in Luke's arms like that. She wouldn't have cared. She probably wouldn't have even noticed.

An echo of Luke's touch reached through the years and surfaced strongly enough for a spiral of desire to clutch something deep within Beth. A sound like a strangled groan escaped her lips and she sank onto a sun-warmed boulder.

How could she cope with this?

It was the ultimate reason to leave, wasn't it? A very clear alarm sounding. If her body and heart were going to rebel against her head and decide they still wanted Luke, then she was going to be vulnerable. She could get hurt.

Again.

The thought was terrifying.

And exhilarating.

The spark was still there. Even if the result was a negative tension, it was better than indifference would have been, wasn't it? When Beth had thought Luke had been ignoring her because he didn't give a damn, she had felt astonishingly let down.

But it hadn't been entirely negative.

He'd told her she'd been brilliant. He had looked at her—for just a fraction of a second—with an expression that had spoken of appreciation. Pride even.

And for the briefest pinpoint of time Beth had felt the sensation of pure joy that had always come from Luke being proud of her. Turning her face up to the sun, Beth closed her eyes and sighed softly. That sensation, however brief, was unforgettable. It was precisely what had been missing from her life for far too long. It was that elusive 'x' factor she had been searching for in all her attempts at other relationships. She had thought she might have found it more than once, only to gather enough doubts to ruin things.

And she'd been so right. Because now that she'd experienced the genuine article again, Beth knew she'd never found anything comparable. The craving to feel it again was undeniably powerful. The fear that she couldn't protect herself if she did was equally strong.

The chance of experiencing it again if she stayed was minimal in any case. Luke hated her now. She was a stranger to him. An angry stranger who confronted people and hated her family. He was clearly bitter about their past. Did he really think that Beth had ended things because she'd thought he Luke 'wasn't good enough'? And how many fiancés did he think she might have had in the intervening years?

It was almost too hard to open her eyes again. It was definitely too confusing to try and make any long-term decisions. Beth needed sleep if she was going to be ready for her next shift tonight.

At Ocean View hospital.

The short-term decision she needed to make was suddenly easy. She wasn't going to leave Hereford just yet. If revisiting her past was too much to handle, how on earth did she imagine she could build herself a future?

Besides, even if she only stayed for a little while, she might find answers to the questions that seemed astonishingly important. If they went unanswered they might haunt her for ever, and the further she moved away from Luke the less likely she would be to ever find those answers.

The minor celebrity status Beth had gained on her inaugural night in Emergency had worn off by the end of her first four night shifts but then, after three days off, she began on days and found it starting all over again.

'I'm Roz,' the red-headed nurse in the locker-room introduced herself. 'And you must be Beth, right? I've heard about you.'

'Oh, no!' Beth grimaced. 'It was a one-off, honestly. I don't go around looking for trouble from gang members. Quite the opposite.'

'Actually, I was talking about the thoracotomy.' Roz closed her locker, smoothed the tunic top of her uniform and gave Beth a curious glance. 'Have you done anything like that before?'

'Hardly. Cracking a chest in an emergency department is not exactly a common procedure, even in big hospitals.'

'First time it's happened here, that's for sure,' Roz

said. 'And it wouldn't have happened at all if it wasn't for Luke. He's amazing, isn't he?'

'He's a good surgeon,' Beth agreed cautiously. She pulled her sweatshirt off and reached into her locker for the dark blue tunic, hoping this wasn't going to be another fishing expedition to gauge whether or not she was attracted to Luke. 'I hear the girl's been discharged from Wellington hospital already.'

Roz nodded again. 'Apparently, she's giving up her gang associations and going home. Being in hospital gave her mother a chance to see her for the first time in years.'

'That's a nice, happy ending. She's been very lucky, having the chance to start again.'

'Thanks to Luke.' Roz was waiting for Beth to lace up the comfortable trainers she wore for work. 'He could have been a cardiothoracic specialist by now—you know, working somewhere like the Mayo Clinic. We're so lucky to have him here.'

The look Beth received implied that she had been lucky to have the opportunity to assist him so closely and it was too good an opening to pass up.

'Really?' Beth's eyebrows rose. 'What made him come and work in a place like Hereford, then?'

'Something to do with his family, I think. I heard he had a sister who died a few years back.'

'Oh?' Beth's response was genuinely surprised.

'And he grew up here.'

Beth had not known that. For a horrible moment she wondered if he *had* told her and the information had been buried in her subconscious, ready to sabotage her after she'd chosen a new place to live. No. He'd talked of Nelson as his childhood stamping ground—a much larger town than Hereford but still not exciting enough for Luke. He hadn't been able to wait to get away…and stay away. Working somewhere like the Mayo Clinic had been right up there on the career ambition list.

Beth shut her locker and then waited as Roz paused in front of the mirror to redo her ponytail and catch errant strands of her long hair.

Losing his only sibling—and a twin at that—would have been dreadful but did it explain the change for someone as determinedly ambitious as Luke had been? Especially when he had never talked about his family in more than general terms. Had he been that close to his sister?

Had it been her own influence that had prevented him sharing that aspect of his life? She had certainly avoided families as a topic of conversation because she'd had no desire to let her own family diminish the joy of being with Luke.

She had made the accusation that it had been Luke's lack of knowledge about her that had caused the failure of their relationship, but how well had *she* actually known Luke?

Surely well enough to guess that the death of a family member wouldn't have been enough to sway the whole direction of his life. There had to be more to it than that but Beth wasn't about to appear too interested by asking questions. If Maureen and Chelsea had a running bet going, how many other staff members would have their antennae up?

Imagine if it got back to Luke that the newest staff member in Emergency appeared to fancy him? The thought was enough to make Beth cringe and she willingly accepted a new topic of conversation as she followed Roz into the department for the 6:45 a.m. staff changeover.

'So, how are you finding work here?'

'It's great.'

'Know your way around now?'

'I'm getting a good handle on the emergency department but I'd still get lost pretty fast if I had to go much further afield.'

'I'm supposed to keep an eye out for you today.' Roz was smiling, apparently happy with the assignment. 'If we get a quiet spell I'll see if can take you on a tour.'

There was to be no quiet spell in the early part of the day. Beth was kept busy monitoring an 84-year-old woman from a local rest home who had a history of cardiac problems and was now developing pneumonia. She required blood tests and X-rays, fluids and antibiotics, and her family needed reassurance that she was getting the best possible care. It was nearly 9 a.m. by the time the elderly woman was transferred to the medical ward and Roz signalled Beth as she returned from accompanying her.

'Would you mind taking the baby in cubicle 3? He's been vomiting all night and I won't be popular if I take a bug home to my boys.'

'Sure.' Beth collected the referral note from the GP. 'How many boys have you got?'

'Five. Six, if you count my husband, Gerry.'

'You're kidding!'

'I wish I was sometimes.'

'How on earth do you manage to find time to work here?'

'I only did one night a week until my youngest, Toby, started school last year. Gerry's very supportive.'

'Five kids!' Beth shook her head, as she moved away. 'That's a big family these days.'

'The first one wasn't exactly planned.' Roz grinned. 'But we figured that since we'd started we might as well carry on. We kept hoping to get a girl eventually.'

'You're not...' Beth stopped speaking as she realised that the question was rather personal, but Roz laughed.

'No. We're not still trying. Have you got any idea what it's like, living with six men? I may as well just nail the toilet seat to the wall.' She pointed towards the IV trolley. 'You'll need to take that. They've sent the baby in because the GP's concerned at her level of dehydration. I'll get one of the docs to come and put it in.'

Beth was still smiling inwardly at the thought of Roz and her toilet seat as she helped the houseman get an IV line into ten-month-old Barry. He was the first child for the anxious mother and Beth did her best to reassure both of them after the young doctor had left to arrange admission.

'Barry's going to be fine, honestly. The worst part's over now that the line is in. He's just going to need watching and some fluid replacement.'

'I just can't bear him being so sick.' Barry's mother was holding him tightly enough to make him protest. Her eyes filled with tears. 'It's awful!'

'He's going to be fine,' Beth repeated. 'Whoops! It might take a while longer for that vomiting to stop. I'll go and a get towel so you can clean up a bit.'

Roz pushed a wheelchair past the linen trolley as Beth collected supplies and she wondered just how many minor or even major crises Roz would have fielded with her tribe of children by now. The feeling of envy was fortunately muted by familiarity but it still stung. Beth was running out of time to hope for much more than one or two children, let alone the big family she had always dreamed of.

Acceptance might have to be the next step. She wouldn't have any children if she wasn't with a partner she truly loved. She had come here to avoid just such a compromise, hadn't she? The notion of a childless future was still not acceptable, however. Beth smiled at Roz. She wasn't going to give up yet. She was only thirty-four, for heaven's sake, and she was in a new place, starting a new life.

She was a whole week into that new life now but Beth had yet to catch another glimpse of Luke. No night time emergencies had occurred that required a surgeon to be called into the department. Disappointingly, it looked as though her first day shift might go the same way.

Having made the decision to stay, Beth had been preparing herself for the next time her path crossed Luke's, quietly confident that she would be able to cope without the confusion and angst that first meeting had sparked. With every passing day she was feeling happier with her decision so why did that knot appear in her stomach when the call for a surgical consult on her next patient was answered…by Luke?

The young girl had come in by ambulance from her school, looking pale and complaining of severe abdominal pain, and Beth hadn't been surprised when the houseman made a provisional diagnosis of appendicitis and referred her to the surgeons.

Luke's smile at Beth, after being introduced to the patient and her mother, was friendly. Professional.

'What's been happening?'

'Katy's had dull, generalised abdominal pain for the last twelve hours.' Beth repeated what the houseman must have already told the surgeon. 'No nausea but she's been anorexic. The pain's settled into the right lower quadrant and she felt too unwell to stay in class this morning. Vital signs are all within normal limits but she's running a mild temperature of 37.4.'

'Got a white-cell count yet?'

'On its way.'

'So, Katy.' Luke's smile for his patient was much warmer than the one Beth had received. 'Got a bit of a sore tummy, huh?'

'It feels better now.'

'Mind if I take a look anyway?'

Luke pressed on the left side of Katy's abdomen first.

'Ow!'

'Where does that hurt?'

'Here.' Close to tears again, Katy pointed to the right side of her abdomen, well away from the pressure.

Luke glanced up. 'Know what that is, Beth?'

'Rovsing's sign.' Beth nodded. 'Associated with rebound tenderness.'

His eyebrow twitched. 'You do know your stuff, don't you? No wonder Mike's been so impressed with you.'

Had the emergency department consultant been talking about her to Luke in the last few days? Was *Luke* impressed? He didn't appear to be.

Neither did Katy's mother. She looked worried.

'What are you talking about? The sign? *Is* it Katy's appendix?'

'It's a definite possibility. Rovsing's sign is one of the things we look for. There are a few other possibilities, though, so we'll need to run a few more tests. Like an ultrasound or CT scan. Beth, could you see if CT is free at the moment?'

'Sure.'

Katy looked frightened. 'Does that hurt?'

'Not a bit, sweetie,' Luke said reassuringly. He rested a hip comfortably on the side of the bed and smiled as Beth slipped out of the cubicle. 'You getting your periods yet, Katy?'

Beth headed for the phone. When had Luke become so comfortable talking to children? Or laid back enough to practically sit on their bed for a comfortable chat? The Luke she had known had always been moving way too fast to pause that long. In far too much of a hurry to get to the top.

This new Luke was even more attractive than the old one. Beth's confidence that she could cope with working in the same place dropped a notch. Possibly two.

Beth's first day shift at Ocean View hospital was almost finished by the time Roz took her on a quick tour.

They bypassed the area adjacent to Emergency that Beth was now familiar with. The minor theatre, Radiology and CT and the plaster room. Roz paused near the pharmacy and small gift shop, manned by volunteers.

'Outpatients is down that corridor. There's also Physiotherapy, Occupational Therapy, Mental Health Services and so on. A few people wander into ED by mistake so it's worth knowing where to direct them.'

Beth peered past Roz. 'It looks busy.'

'It always is. Hereford's only small but the hospital has a huge catchment area.'

'That explains why the staff is so much bigger than I'd expected. I must say I was surprised. I'd expected this quiet little small town hospital.' The number of staff hadn't been the real surprise, though, had it? More the calibre. 'I'm still amazed at how many consultants there are.'

'Yes, we have a lot. The private work fills in any slack time but there seems to be less and less of that these days.'

'There are private patients?' Beth couldn't hide her astonishment.

'Just one ward. It's shared by all the consultants doing private work. They use the hospital facilities and I guess the insurance companies pay the government. The consultants and anaesthetists get a separate fee, of course.'

'Of course. I suppose Luke Savage does most of the private work?'

'What makes you say that?'

'I…um…' Beth bit her lip. What *had* made her say that? Because fame and fortune had been so important to the man she'd known? Because his desire to become a kind of clone of her father had started the rapid downhill slide of their relationship? The fact that private work was available had seemed like another small piece to fit into the puzzle of why Luke was here, but the expression on her colleague's face was making her wonder now. 'I have no idea,' she concluded lamely. 'It just seemed to fit.'

'Weird.' Roz shook her head. 'He's the only surgeon who *doesn't* do private work. Len does any general stuff and the orthopaedic guys share out the hip replacements and so on.'

'Is that the maternity ward?' Beth was eager to change the subject.

'Yes. And that's Paediatrics beside it.'

Beth latched onto a good way to distract Roz. 'My sister's a paediatrician. In Sydney.'

'Really?'

'And I've got a brother who's a cardiologist in London.'

'Wow. That's a very medical family.'

'Mmm.' Beth suddenly regretted the change of subject because the look Roz was giving her was rather too familiar. Maybe Luke hadn't spread the interesting information about her background any further.

'Dawson…you're not related to *Nigel* Dawson, are you? That heart surgeon guy?'

Beth suppressed a groan. 'He's my father.'

'Wow!'

Beth shrugged her eyebrows. Despite the feeling that she and Roz could end up being good friends, she wasn't about to start spilling the beans about how her father's personality and career had had such an adverse effect on her family and childhood.

'I read about him not so long ago,' Roz continued. 'Isn't your mother medical as well?'

'An anaesthetist,' Beth confirmed. 'They met in a theatre and have worked together ever since.'

'How romantic!'

'Mmm.' Was it romantic to allow nothing, including three children, to interfere in any way with accruing fame and fortune?

'And you went into *nursing*?'

'I'm the black sheep,' Beth confessed lightly.

Roz laughed. 'Every family should have one, I guess. Do you know where the surgical ward is?'

Beth nodded. 'I went up with Katy when she got admitted for surgery.'

Luke hadn't been there. And Beth had been irritated with herself at finding that disappointing.

'OK. I'll show you the really important stuff now, like the staff swimming pool. You'll be diving in like the rest of us at the end of every shift in summer, believe me.'

'I love swimming,' Beth said, 'but I prefer the beach.'

'You'd better talk to Luke, then.'

Beth's spine prickled as her pulse quickened. 'Why?'

'He lives on the most perfect beach around these parts. Boulder Bay. You'll have to wangle an invitation and try swimming there. It's gorgeous.'

'But New Zealand has public access to any beach. They can't be private.'

'It's not, but you need four-wheel drive to get up and down the access road safely. Have you got a four-wheel-drive vehicle?'

'No.'

'So that's why you'll need to talk to Luke. He won't mind giving you a lift if you leave your car at the top of the hill. That's what we all do. Look, that's him just over there. I could ask him for you, if you're shy.'

Beth laughed. 'No, thanks. I can do my own asking. He looks a bit busy right now.'

He was talking to a woman who had just emerged from the pharmacy and was looking into the contents of a paper bag. She was an attractive blonde, probably in her late twenties, and the diamond rings on her left hand caught the light as she moved. Whoever she was, and despite her obvious marital status, she had Luke's full attention.

'I'm just going to grab a chocolate bar from the gift shop,' Roz said. 'Want something?'

Beth shook her head. 'No, thanks. I'll just wait here.'

Where she could appear to be admiring the display of flowers and teddy bears for sale while Roz waited in a small queue. Where she could still see Luke talking to the pretty blonde.

The woman seemed to be scrubbing tears from her face when Beth flicked a glance in her direction. Was she the relative of a patient perhaps? She saw the blonde nodding as though whatever Luke was saying was what she needed to hear. Then she saw Luke's arm going around the woman's shoulders and the impression of closeness touched a very deep chord in Beth. This was no professional relationship. She would never believe that Luke would be having an affair with a married woman, but whoever the blonde was, she had a bond with Luke that clearly meant a lot to them both.

And it hurt, dammit! There was no way Beth could reason her way out of this reaction. Had she really thought she could cope? This was jealousy, pure and simple. A nasty feeling that Beth wanted to eliminate as quickly as possible. Roz was finally paying for her chocolate. Beth moved to meet her at the door of the shop. A rapid escape seemed entirely possible.

Until Luke called out. And waved. And came towards her.

'We got to Katy's appendix just in time,' he told Beth. 'It looked like it wasn't that far off perforating.'

'That's good.' Beth edged closer to the door. She didn't want to talk to Luke. Not while she was struggling with the knowledge that she still cared enough to be jealous of any other potential women in Luke's life.

Luke's smile hadn't lost any of its charm. 'Look, I'm sorry about the other night. I shouldn't have said anything to Mike about your father. I really don't want to make a new start any more difficult for you.'

'It doesn't matter,' Beth muttered ungraciously. It was on the tip of her tongue to say something about how hard it was to escape the past no matter how much you might want to but fortunately, perhaps, Luke spoke again first.

'We should have a coffee one of these days, Beth, and catch up on the last few years.'

He was being so *friendly*. Casual. As though she was simply an old acquaintance and it really didn't matter if they 'caught up' or not. The evil claws of jealousy were still digging into Beth and they sharpened her tone far more than she liked.

'I came here for a change of lifestyle, Luke. I don't see much point in raking up the past.'

'Fair enough.' The upward inflection on the last word was subtle but nevertheless conveyed that Luke had received the message. He wouldn't be making another attempt to engage Beth socially in a hurry. 'See you around, then.'

Roz emerged from the gift shop and received a smile from Luke warm enough to highlight just how chilly his words to Beth had been.

'Hiya, Roz. Sorry, I can't stop and chat just now. We'll have to catch up soon with a coffee or something. Everything all right with that tribe of boys you live with?'

'Great, thanks. You'll have to come to dinner soon.'

'Love to.' And Luke was gone with a friendly wave to Roz and not even a glance back at Beth.

Beth straightened her spine. She didn't care. Luke would probably be avoiding her from now on and that should make things a lot easier.

She should be happy.

'Are you all right?' Roz was giving her a curious look.

Beth pasted a smile to her face. 'I'm fine, really. Just a bit tired.'

'Me, too. It's been a busy day.' Roz nodded her understanding and smiled back, clearly convinced that Beth was being honest.

It was just a shame she couldn't convince herself so easily.

CHAPTER FOUR

THE cigarette was ground out in the gravel of Ocean View hospital's car park with an angry gesture and the pretty blonde woman sighed heavily as she climbed into the black Jeep.

'I've just wasted my money, haven't I? On those nicotine patches?'

'Consider it an investment.' Luke smiled. 'They'll keep.'

Maree Winsome sighed again. 'I'm hopeless, aren't I? My brother is dying of lung cancer and I can't give up smoking.'

'Kev's cancer has nothing to do with cigarettes. You know he's never smoked in his life. The pancreas was the site of the primary tumour. It's just spread to his lungs.'

'I know. It's so bloody unfair. It should be *me*.'

'Don't be daft. Life is often very unfair. We both know that.'

Maree broke the silence after Luke started the vehicle and moved off. 'This is really hard on you, too, isn't it? You and Kev have always been so close.'

'We've been best mates since we met at play centre

when we were about three. The terrible duo, they used to call us.'

Maree smiled. 'I used to get so jealous of Jodie because she got to hang out with you guys. Did you know I had a huge crush on you when I was, like, twelve or thirteen?'

'No kidding? No, I never knew that.' Luke grinned. 'Does John know about this?'

'Of course. I was well over it by the time I met him.'

'How is John?'

'He's fine. A bit worried about me. He's coming over for the weekend and he said he's looking forward to catching up with you.'

'I haven't seen John since…' Luke had to clear his throat. 'Hell, I haven't seen him since Jodie's funeral— just before you guys moved to Sydney.'

'And I met him at Jodie and Kev's wedding.' Maree's smile was poignant. 'Small world, isn't it?'

'It's smaller when you come from a place like this.' Luke headed uphill and turned into a tree-lined avenue.

'I miss it sometimes,' Maree said. 'Part of it, anyway. Not that I'd want to live here again. I like the pace of city life too much.'

'I used to think like that. I'd never have come back for more than a few days' visit if Jodie hadn't got sick. And then I kept coming back because I couldn't stay away.'

'And now you wouldn't live anywhere else, huh?'

'It's home,' Luke agreed simply.

Maree nodded. 'I'd forgotten how much like an extended family a small community can be when you need support. Two of the neighbours turned up with casseroles last night and old Mr Donaghue from the end of the road came and mowed the lawns today without even being asked. And Mum would have no hope of coping with any of this if it wasn't for your mum, Luke. She's practically living at our house.'

Luke pulled up in front of the old villa that badly needed a coat of paint as she spoke. 'That's what best friends are for.'

'She's amazing. And it must be *so* hard. I know it's been four years but it must be bringing back so many memories of Jodie. For all of you.'

'The memories have always been there. Kev was never able to let go.'

Maree made no move to get out of the car. Her face was serious. 'Do you think that's made a difference, Luke? I mean, he hasn't put up any kind of a fight, has he?' She didn't wait for a response. 'It's makes me so angry sometimes. What right has he got to just give up the will to live? Do his family and friends not count for anything?'

'We count,' Luke said gently. 'But it isn't our battle, love. All we can do is be here for him and help in any way he wants us to.'

'Well, I don't want to help him die.' Fresh tears rolled down Maree's cheeks and she wrenched the car door open and then slammed it shut behind her. She turned away from the house, however, reaching into her handbag for her packet of cigarettes. 'You go on,' she instructed Luke. 'I need a few minutes to pull myself together.'

'Want some company?'

'You want to make me feel even guiltier by subjecting you to secondhand smoke?' Maree managed a watery smile. 'No. Go away, Luke. Kev's been asking for you. You go and do the visiting thing.'

It was no surprise for Luke to find his own mother completely at home and busy in Joan Winsome's kitchen but, then, this house had always been a second home for him. The two families had been linked long before Kevin and Luke had become inseparable friends. Luke's father, Don, had been more than an honorary uncle to the Winsome children after Joan's husband had died when Maree had been a baby.

The tragically brief marriage between Kevin and Luke's twin sister, Jodie, had only deepened an already unbreakable bond, and Luke's mother, Barbara, and Joan Winsome were closer than sisters. The twist of fate that was putting them through the unbearable pain of losing another young life was appallingly unfair but Luke knew they would get through this by leaning on each other.

They all would. There was simply no other choice.

The hug Luke gave his mother conveyed that message well enough for her to nod as she pulled away. And to smile.

'Did Maree find you? She walked into the hospital to collect the morphine prescription.'

'I gave her a ride home. She's outside at the moment beating herself up over her smoking.'

Barbara sighed. 'I'll go and talk to her. She's quite stressed enough right now, without putting herself through any more. She's been feeling too sick to eat properly for days now.'

'I know. It's tough all round, isn't it?'

'I persuaded Joannie to lie down for a while. She got really upset when Kev decided to plan the music for his funeral.'

Luke groaned softly. 'Oh, no!'

'He's been asking when you were coming. He's got a list of CDs he wants to borrow. Said he can't guarantee he'll give them back, though.'

Luke was still shaking his head, smiling, as he went through to the sunroom at the closed-in end of the villa's long verandah. That was so like his mate, to be making jokes to try and lighten such a bleak atmosphere. Jodie had died in her husband's arms when she'd succumbed to the vicious form of leukaemia she had contracted, and Kevin swore she had been still smiling at the last joke he'd told her.

'Hey, Kev.' Luke sat down on one of the chairs beside the bed that the palliative care department of Ocean View had provided. The electronic adjustments could be varied enough to provide comfort and the soft cushioning of the inflatable mattress cover and the sheepskins was a bonus. 'What's all this I hear about the concert you're planning?'

Eyes too large for a wasted face were fixed on Luke. 'Is Mum still upset, then?'

'I haven't seen her. She's asleep, I think. Anything I can get for you, buddy?'

'Yeah. Your retro CD…that's got Procul Harem… "Whiter Shade of Pale"?' Kevin Winsome's lung capacity was reduced enough now for him to need to catch his breath after every few words. 'Nice and ghostly…huh?'

'It's no wonder your mum's upset, mate. You just can't stop stirring, can you?'

'I'll stop soon enough.' Kevin smiled slowly. 'And then you'll…be sorry.'

'Yeah.' Luke couldn't keep up the banter. Maybe Maree was right. Kevin was too accepting of all this.

'What I meant was, did you need a drink or some more jungle juice or something? How's the pain?'

Kevin's hand movement was weak but still dismissive. 'We've got better…things to talk…about. Can you…make a list…for me? Of songs?'

What had Luke just said to Maree? That all they could do was to help in any way Kevin wanted them to? 'Sure thing,' he said softly. He pulled out the notepad and pencil that he always kept in his shirt pocket. 'Fire away,' he instructed Kevin. 'What's first?'

'That soppy one that…Jodie chose for our…wedding song.'

Luke's gaze went to the most prominent photograph in the clutter of pictures lining the window-sill beside Kevin. His sister had been the happiest bride in the world, no question. Thank God none of them had known she would be diagnosed with a fatal illness within a year.

Kevin had followed Luke's line of vision. 'Gorgeous, isn't she?'

Luke nodded, the lump in his throat precluding speech.

'I could never…have found anyone…to take her place…you know.'

'You two were soul mates, that's for sure.'

'Not many people…are that lucky.' Kevin was tiring and had to catch his breath several times before he could speak again. Then he caught Luke's gaze. 'I'm not afraid…to die, mate… I'm kind of hoping…to see Jodie…again.'

Luke's mouth twisted. 'You'll have to say hi from me, then. I miss her.'

'You have to find…your soul mate…otherwise I'll come back…and haunt you.'

'I'm being haunted already, thanks. You remember that theatre nurse I was planning to marry? Beth Dawson?'

Kevin's nod was painfully slow. 'She's the only one...who ever made you...think about getting...married.'

'Well, she's turned up here. Taken a job in the emergency department at Ocean View.'

'Why?'

'That's what I'd like to know.'

'Is she...married now?'

'I don't know. She's not wearing any rings but she might just take them off for work.'

'Ask her.'

'I can't do that. Can't ask anyone else either. You know what hospital gossip is like. She might think I was interested in her again.'

'You are.'

'No way. She dumped me, remember?'

'You didn't try very hard...to fix things, mate.'

'I wasn't going to beg her to take me back, if that's what you mean. There were plenty of others who wanted to play. Anyway, it's all water under the bridge and I don't want to go swimming in that particular river again. Neither does she.'

'How do you...know that?'

'I met her in the corridor this afternoon and she gave me a look that would have curdled milk. The woman still loathes me.'

'Flip the coin.'

'What?'

'Hate's just...the other side of...love, isn't it?'

'You're getting a bit philosophical in your old age, aren't you?'

'May as well.' Kevin was giving Luke a very intense look. 'She still cares… You could find…a way to flip…the coin if…you wanted.'

'Doubt it.' Luke grinned. 'Beth has her foot on that coin very firmly. I don't think she has any intention of even speaking to me again.'

'I have no intention of *ever* speaking to him again.'

'You'll have to at some point. You work in the same hospital.'

'Maybe I won't stay after all. I could learn to make cappuccinos, Neroli. Surely your sister could take on another waitress or something?'

'You don't want to do that.'

'Why not? You're having fun, aren't you?'

'I think the novelty's starting to wear off.' A sigh echoed over the phone line. 'I really miss nursing. I think I might have overreacted by chucking it in. I could have just made a change from the emergency department. I'd quite like to be a theatre nurse, actually.'

'Good thinking. The patients are knocked out so they can't give you any grief. And you never know your luck. You might even meet a hot surgeon!'

They both laughed but then it was Beth's turn to sigh. She was staring at her feet. 'I'm wearing those rabbit slipper socks you gave me for Christmas last year.' If she wiggled her toes the whiskers on the bright pink rabbit faces twitched and the ears that were attached near her ankles bent forward as though listening to something interesting. Beth smiled. 'I really miss having you around, Neroli. I could use a best friend.'

'Luke could be your best friend if you gave him a chance.'

'Have you not heard a word I've said?' Beth clicked her tongue sadly. 'I shudder to think how much I've spent on this phone call already and now I have to tell you all over again. I'm curious about the man, not *interested* in him.'

'Doesn't sound like it from this side of the ditch, chick. I think you're jea—'

'Good grief!' Beth interrupted. 'What the hell was *that*?'

'What *is* that?' Neroli's voice was very faint as Beth held the phone at arm's length so she could see out the window. 'Sounds like someone's screaming. Beth? Beth? Are you all right?'

'Got to go. Looks like someone's come off their motorbike just outside.' She didn't wait to hear her friend's farewell. She didn't even stop long enough to change the fluffy slipper socks, but nobody seemed to notice as she arrived at the scene of the accident seconds later.

'Beth!' The woman from the dairy opposite the motel had learned her name within a week of her arrival. Beth had liked the friendly interest from the shopkeeper. 'Thank goodness. You're a nurse, aren't you?'

'Did you see what happened?'

'He shot round that corner and just went straight into the lamppost. Is he dead?'

'No.' Beth could feel a good carotid pulse. The black helmet the youth was wearing seemed undamaged but his left leg was bleeding and one arm was bent at an unnatural angle. Right now, though, Beth was more concerned about his breathing. And his neck. 'Has someone called for an ambulance?'

'I did.' The man was still holding the carton of milk he had obviously purchased in the dairy. 'It's on its way.'

'And isn't that Dr Savage?'

'What?' Beth lost count of both the respiratory and pulse rate she had been trying to take simultaneously.

'What kind of name is that for a doctor?' The man with the milk sounded incredulous.

Beth almost smiled. Luke had said exactly the same thing once. 'And I'm not savage,' he'd added with a winning smile. 'Am I?'

And Beth had assured him he was anything but. Determined, yes. Confident, certainly, but she hadn't thought it tipped over into arrogance. Not then, anyway. Ruthless? Unlikely. But very definitely not savage. He was capable, in fact, of being the most gentle man Beth had ever known. She opened her mouth to say something in defence of Luke and his name but there was no need.

'He's a wonderful doctor,' the woman from the dairy informed her customer stoutly. 'He looked after my dad last year and you wouldn't want anyone else after you've had Dr Savage, let me tell you. You'd know all about that, wouldn't you, Beth?'

The groan was fortunately contained in her head. Luke had slammed the door of the sleek black Jeep behind him and had clearly heard the final piece of that interchange. His startled glance at Beth set a confused whirl of thoughts into that spin-drier action again.

You wouldn't want anyone else after you've had Dr Savage.

The comment stabbed at something astonishingly raw. Neroli had been about to tell her she was jealous of that blonde woman she had seen in Luke's company. And it was true. She *was* jealous. And she had never found anyone she truly wanted after Luke. Imagine if she'd agreed with the woman from the dairy? Both she and Luke would know she wasn't referring to any professional skills the man possessed, however wonderful they were.

Again, thankfully, there was no need or opportunity for her to say anything. Luke's glance had been even briefer than the painful flash of insight. He was now crouched beside the young man on the road.

'Airway's clear,' Beth told him. 'But I haven't been able to assess his breathing properly with the way he's lying.' The crumpled figure was almost in a recovery position and while she could feel the movement of his chest and abdomen, it was hardly adequate for a proper assessment.

'We've got enough people to do a log roll.' Luke moved to hold the helmeted head. 'I'll look after his neck.' He looked up at the bystanders. 'You're Mrs Coulter, aren't you?'

'Doris.' The woman from the dairy beamed at the recognition.

'I need you to help us, Doris. We're going to turn this man over so he's lying on his back but we need to be very careful with his neck. We'll need you as well,' he told the man with the milk. 'Beth will show you where to put your hands.'

It took only moments to achieve spinal alignment and the movement made the injured man groan.

'It's OK,' Luke told him. 'Try not to move, mate. You've had an accident. Can you open your eyes?'

The groan was louder this time but there was no response to the command. Luke frowned, adjusting his hold on the man's head. 'Stay as still as you can,' he instructed. 'Beth, can you undo that jacket? OK, chest wall movement looks equal from here.'

Beth nodded. 'I can't feel any rib fractures. Sternum feels stable and trachea looks midline.'

'What's happening with that leg? Looks like there's some blood loss that needs controlling.'

The wail of a siren was getting steadily closer as Beth removed the now bloodsoaked blanket Doris had helpfully fetched and then used to cover the lower half of the injured man.

'Looks like a degloving injury.' Beth eyed the mangled skin and flesh dubiously. 'I can't see any obvious fracture.'

'Use that towel that Doris has to cover it.' The ambulance was pulling to a halt and Luke was watching for the paramedic to emerge. 'Sally—good to see you. We need some large dressings, stat. I didn't have my first-aid kit on me.'

Sally's partner put an oxygen cylinder on its side near Luke and attached a high-concentration mask to the outlet.

'Can you grab a collar, please?' Luke asked him. 'And, Beth, could you help me get his helmet off so we can put a collar on? Sally can deal with that leg. She's got gloves on.'

They should all have gloves on, Beth realised. She slipped hands that already had smears of blood on them inside the bike helmet to hold the youth's head as Luke gently eased the bulky item clear. His movements were very careful and he was making very sure he didn't move the man's neck as he removed the helmet.

It was inevitable that their hands would touch. And not just briefly. At one point Luke's hands overlaid Beth's as he inched the helmet clear with tiny increments of zigzagging pressure from his thumbs. Every second of that physical contact seemed to Beth to stretch into infinity. The effect of the most fleeting touch that night of the thoracotomy had been noticeable and they had both been wearing gloves that night.

This was bare flesh against bare flesh and the nerves in Beth's hands had caught fire. The burning sensation was travelling up her arms and then spiralling down to somewhere deep in her abdomen.

'Right. Keep holding that position, Beth, until we get the collar into place.'

Things seemed to happen fast after that. Too fast. The injured man was given oxygen. An IV line was inserted. His level of consciousness was improving rapidly as his leg was covered with sterile dressings and then a pressure bandage put on to control the bleeding. His neck was encased in a semi-rigid collar and then he was strapped to a backboard, with cushions and straps ensuring that no untoward movement could worsen a neck injury.

Within fifteen minutes they were ready to load and Luke was heading for his vehicle.

'I'll go in with him,' he told Beth. 'He's going to need that leg cleaned out under anaesthetic. Do you want a lift home?'

'No. I'm living just across the road.'

'Really? You're lucky. Places this close to the beach don't come up very often.'

'I'm in the motel.' Beth felt inexplicably embarrassed and dropped her gaze. It felt like she was admitting some kind of failure. She was a displaced person with no home. 'Just temporarily.'

'Oh-h.' The drawn-out monosyllable had an odd tone to it. Beth glanced up but could then see why Luke sounded odd. He was staring at her feet and Beth blushed.

'They were a present,' she muttered. 'From a good friend.'

'Very cute.' Luke looked up and caught her gaze. And then he smiled. Beth smiled back and for just a moment there was a connection of shared amusement. And then, suddenly, there was a much deeper connection and their smiles dimmed as quickly as if a switch had been flicked.

And they both turned away at precisely the same moment. The ambulance edged past and Sally was looking out of the driver's window.

'Shall I tell them you're on your way, Luke?'

'I'll be right behind you.' Luke got into his vehicle and drove away. Beth had no idea whether he looked back or said goodbye because she was walking back to her motel unit and she did not turn back.

At least, not until his car was just a black speck at the far end of the road.

Daytime shifts at Ocean View were busy enough to leave Beth little time to think about personal issues, which was just as well because she seemed to see rather a lot of Luke over the next four shifts.

Did he never have days off? Why didn't he send a registrar or houseman down when surgical opinions were sought in the emergency department?

And how did a population base as small as that which Ocean View serviced manage to produce so many patients requiring the skills of a general surgeon? There had been two cases of obstructed bowels and a perforated duodenal ulcer. A baby had come in with a Meckel's diverticulum and there had been an elderly man whose colostomy had broken down. Then there had been a case of rectal cancer, a femoral hernia and a nasty abscess or two.

Beth counted them off on her fingers. OK, so Luke hadn't appeared to assess them all but he *had* appeared in the department at least once every day. There had also been the times she had spotted him in the staff cafeteria and he had driven past her when she had been walking home yesterday. There was simply no way to avoid the accumulation of reactions that required considerable thought when she had her quiet moments away from the hospital.

None of those occasions had provoked more turmoil than the encounter on Tuesday evening, however. It had been a long and very hot day and Roz had persuaded Beth to have a quick swim in the hospital pool before heading home.

'But I don't have any swimming togs.'

'Chelsea keeps some in her locker. She won't mind if you borrow them.'

And Chelsea had arrived for her night shift and agreed wholeheartedly. 'Go for it,' she'd urged Beth. 'My togs should fit you.'

They had, though rather too snugly for Beth's comfort. She had never been a stick figure but the cut of the costume had given her a cleavage that had made her wish she'd had a T-shirt available to wear on top. At least it had been black, which had helped the hip line, but Beth had regretted her decision to swim the instant she had surfaced from her first dive into the deliciously cool water.

Luke was dropping a towel onto one of the deck chairs surrounding the pool. His swimming shorts were boxer style and hardly revealing, but Beth's memory banks happily filled in the area covered by the modest costume and suddenly the water lost any of its power to cool and soothe.

Like his face, the whole of Luke's body was browner and leaner than it had been six years ago. There wasn't an ounce of fat to blur the outline of muscle on those long, long legs and broad shoulders. The evening sun gave his bronzed skin a warm glow and Beth had to duck below the surface of the water to stop herself staring.

Luke was still, by far, the most gorgeous man she had ever met.

Going underwater was her second mistake of the evening. She had to come up for air eventually and it was unfortunate that her timing and position coincided with Luke completing his initial dive. He surfaced close enough for Beth to be liberally splashed by the water he shook from his head and she could almost feel those long fingers as they raked hair back from his forehead and out of his eyes.

'I sure need a haircut.' Luke blinked droplets from the thick, dark eyelashes Beth had once coveted, and then his gaze focussed. 'Oh…hi, Beth.'

'Hi.' Being below the surface for so long had left her breathless. Beth trod water but the sight of Luke's near-naked body scrambled her brain and she was totally unable to think of anything else to say.

'Hey, Luke!' Roz was waving a large Frisbee. 'Catch!'

He did and then he flung the Frisbee back to Roz, who immediately flicked it on to Beth. She missed, thanks to her reluctance to launch herself any closer to Luke, but then she caught the mood of the group of people intent on having as good a time as possible as they cooled off and her own agenda could be shoved aside.

It was fun. Seeing Luke's glistening body as he leapt and dived as enthusiastically as anyone else was simply a part of that enjoyment. Beth even decided that the wayward reaction her own body was producing was simply another memory that hadn't been adequately filed.

The mental filing proved difficult, however. It was easy enough to locate the pocket it should go in once Beth was alone later that evening, but the temptation to ruffle through other memories of Luke's body proved too powerful.

The way he had kissed her. No, the way he had looked at her *before* he had kissed her. As though she had been the only thing in the universe that Luke had been aware of. The only thing that had mattered. His hands would cradle her head so gently and Beth would watch his eyes and then his lips as he started to slowly close the distance between them. And Beth would be in freefall, the anticipation and excitement and sheer driving lust making her as completely focussed on Luke as he was on her.

The memory had been enough all by itself to stir a physical reaction that could only leave pure frustration in its wake. Beth had shoved the memory back, thrown in the one of Luke in the swimming pool and tried to slam the drawer shut on the mental filing cabinet. She had tried *very* hard.

And yesterday, Wednesday, she had avoided even looking at Luke when he'd been in the department, in case that drawer broke a lock she knew was weak and started sliding open. She had kept her head down and repeated very firmly to herself that nothing had changed.

Just because he was still such an attractive man didn't

change a thing. The fact that her relationship with Luke had been enough to sour any later attempts to connect to other men also changed nothing. Luke Savage was *not* the man she needed in her life right now. She was not going to go down that road again no matter what Neroli thought because she knew there was an accident scene at the other end of the road and that the victim would be herself.

She didn't need Luke in her life. She didn't need any man in her life. At least, not until she had sorted herself out a little more. No wonder her relationships in the last few years had never worked out. How could she hope to be happy with someone else if she wasn't happy with herself?

What she needed, Beth decided, was a focus that was purely selfish. Something that would keep her busy outside working hours. Busy enough to get past the mental block Luke had presented. Heavens, if she kept up thinking about the man this much, she would have to admit it was becoming an obsession and that would be totally unacceptable. Pathetic, even.

Beth used her days off to search for that new focus. One of the benefits of living in a motel was the wealth of pamphlets available that extolled all the attractions of the area she was now living in. On her first days off after the night shifts, Beth travelled the short distance to the Marlborough Sounds and she fell in love with the seemingly infinite number of sheltered bays and islands. The wildlife cruise she took let her see tiny blue penguins for the first time and almost touch a dolphin that cruised on her side of the shallow boat.

There were plenty more attractions. Hereford was a town in an area now famous for its vineyards and crafts. There were fabulous restaurants to try, gardens to visit, riverboat cruises and the most wonderful shopping at numerous craft galleries and markets. Beth set out to explore and found herself tasting treats like early cherries, asparagus and crayfish caught just down the coast at Kaikoura. She made plans to attend the upcoming wine and food festival that was now a major attraction for Marlborough, and she stopped her car on several occasions just to admire the views.

She loved it all. The sea and forests, the hills and mountains. She loved the fabulous climate and the casual way people dressed. The way Doris from the dairy always greeted her by name and the wonderful sunsets she was in the habit of watching from a now favourite boulder on the beach near the motel.

What she didn't love was the motel unit and the way the walls closed in on her when she had to return to sleep, but on her second day off Beth found the answer. She had started making an effort to stop at every tiny craft gallery she passed in her explorations the previous day but she almost missed this one. The hand-painted sign advertising pottery was only just visible beneath the ivy creeping up its pole. The shop was just as low key— part of a shed that housed the artist's kiln.

But there it was. The Answer. Staring at Beth in the form of a casserole dish. The pottery was gorgeous. With a base colour of a rich, earthy brown, a golden-hued glaze had been applied so that it looked as if something had boiled over and oozed down the sides to finally trickle into droplets that ringed the base like jewels. What really captured Beth, however, was not the piece of pottery so much as what it represented.

Home. An oven from which the aroma of a hot, meaty dinner wafted on a cold winter's night. A family big enough to warrant cooking the size of casserole this dish would hold. A table big enough for them all to gather around. Beth could almost hear the laughter and feel the love around that table, and the yearning was strong enough to be painful.

That was what she wanted in her life. What she had always wanted even when she had been too young to understand what had been missing. Waiting for the right partner to provide a home was never going to work. And it didn't matter because Beth could do it for herself. Well, maybe not the family bit but she could certainly do the rest.

'I'll take this dish, please,' she told the owner of the kiln. 'I just love it. And you wouldn't happen to know any local real estate agents, would you?'

The first step was taken late the same afternoon and it was with a sense of growing excitement that Beth found herself being chauffeured around Hereford by Ronald from L. J. Homes Ltd, viewing any available properties within easy commuting distance of Ocean View hospital.

'I'd like something old,' she told Ronald. 'I'd be happy to renovate.' Restoring an old house would be a wonderful project to keep her occupied outside work, wouldn't it? And it would be a home. A real home. She would spend all the money she had saved so carefully ever since she had started working. She would buy at least part of the dream symbolised by the casserole dish that was now looking oddly out of place on the tiny kitchenette bench of her motel unit.

'I'd really like to be near the beach,' she added.

'Might be a bit pricey for you, love.' Ronald consulted a printout of listed properties he had in his briefcase. 'We could get you up on the hills maybe, with a *view* of the sea. Or what about south of town, near the river?'

Beth was looking at the printout as well. 'That cottage looks cute. Can I see that first?'

So they drove a little north of Hereford. Ronald's car slowed to negotiate the bend at the top of a hill and Beth turned her head sharply to peer at the yellow wooden arrow on her side of the road.

'So that's where Boulder Bay is!' she exclaimed.

'Do you know it?'

'I've heard of it.' Beth wished she hadn't sounded so interested. To have any thoughts of Luke encroaching on this new adventure took some of the excitement away.

'Nothing for sale down there,' Ronald told her. 'And even if there was, you couldn't afford it, I'm afraid. Besides, the road's awful and the residents aren't going to pay for it to get upgraded. They like their privacy.'

'How many houses are down there?'

'Only one.' Ronald was increasing speed as the road led down the other side of the hill. 'Belongs to one of the docs at the hospital. You said you were a nurse, right?'

'Yes.'

'You probably know the bloke, then. Luke Savage?'

'I've met him.' Beth's tone prompted a glance from Ronald who instantly dropped the subject and left them in silence until he pulled up outside the cottage Beth wanted to view.

Not that she took that much notice of the tour. Ronald had said 'they'. If there was more than one resident to the exclusive Boulder Bay, it had to mean that Luke was sharing his house.

Who with? The woman wearing the wedding ring? No. Beth actually shook her head. It simply didn't fit.

Ronald had noticed the unconscious gesture. 'Not what you're looking for?'

'Not really.'

'Right. Let's try something else, then. There's a house not too far from here. We might as well have a look while we're on this side of town.'

Beth took more notice of this property but it was an isolated cottage and so rundown it would be a daunting prospect to renovate. She loved the acre of land that came with it, however, and spent some time exploring the sheds. It was Ronald who called it a day.

'It's getting late,' he reminded Beth. 'I'd like to drive you past another place while there's still enough day-light to see. And then I'd better get you home.'

But Beth wasn't quite ready to go back to the sterile motel unit.

'I might walk,' she told Ronald. 'Can you drop me at the top of the hill?'

'It'll take you hours.'

'It's only a few kilometres. I often walk for an hour or more on my days off. I could do with the exercise.'

'If you're sure.' Ronald stopped the car but looked dubious. 'It's going to get dark before you get home.'

'I'm sure. Thanks very much for your time, Ronald. I'll have a think about those houses and call you tomorrow.'

The walk would be a good time to think and Beth really did want some vigorous exercise. It wasn't until the taillights of Ronald's car blinked as he slowed further down the hill that she realised just where she had requested the stop. Her breath left her lungs in an incredulous huff as she saw the yellow arrow sign.

Boulder Bay.

How far would she have to walk down the road in

order to see the house Luke lived in? Beth's steps slowed but didn't stop. No. It would be just too embarrassing if he caught her acting like some sort of stalker.

But was the beach as beautiful as Roz had told her? And what sort of house did Luke live in? Ten days ago Beth would have been quite confident that any real estate Luke purchased would have to be an architectural statement that advertised status. If it was, maybe the mystery of why Luke had compromised his career to such a degree would be solved. Had he been so successful already that he was in a kind of early retirement?

The thought was intriguing enough to make Beth stop. Just a quick look to satisfy her curiosity, she decided. With a rapid scan for traffic, Beth almost scuttled across the road and set off towards Boulder Bay at a brisk pace. Twenty minutes later she could see the outlines of a house set into the cliffside at the far end of a picture-perfect bay, despite the light fading more rapidly than she had expected. There were no lights on. Maybe Luke had been held up at work. He could be sitting on a deck, enjoying the sunset, or maybe he used this part of his day to wander on what had to be almost a private beach.

And no wonder it had been named for its boulders. The white sand of the beach gleamed in the soft light but only small pathways towards the water were visible. Enormous boulders ringed the beach and were strewn across the sand. Beth had never seen such huge, smooth black rocks. And how come they glistened as though they were wet when the conditions were far too calm to have thrown any spray that far?

Puzzled, Beth walked a little further. Then she stopped abruptly, put her hand up to shield her eyes from the last rays of sun for the day and she stared intently at the beach.

It had to have been her imagination.

But then it happened again.

One of the boulders *moved*.

And then a jet of spray of water coming from another of the enormous rocks caught enough light to resemble a tiny fountain and an odd, mournful sound carried clearly up the hill to where Beth finally realised what she was seeing.

Whales.

She had heard of mass strandings, of course. Had seen pictures of people fighting to save the huge mammals on more than one occasion but Beth had no idea what to do right now.

She had to call help and find someone who *did* know. How long would it take her to run back uphill and then find a telephone? Who would she call? The police maybe?

Beth was in the process of turning to retrace her steps when her peripheral vision caught something and she turned back and then breathed a sigh of relief.

A light had come on at Luke's house. He was home and he would know what to do.

Keeping to the side of the gravel road where the grass verge gave more secure footing, Beth began to run downhill.

Towards Boulder Bay beach.

Towards Luke's home.

CHAPTER FIVE

'WHAT the—?'

Luke braked sharply enough to cause a slight skid in the loose shingle of the road leading to his home as his headlights picked out the solitary figure running down the verge.

Being the back view of a person in an unnaturally bright spotlight was no hindrance to recognition, and Luke knew exactly who it was almost instantly.

At least this time the curvy figure was fully clothed. The last time Luke had seen Beth out of uniform had been at the staff swimming pool on Tuesday, and the image of her body in a swimsuit that had to be a size too small had been plaguing him ever since.

Not that that had stopped him frequenting the emergency department of Ocean View far more often than was customary. If anything, he was even less able to resist that magnetic 'scab-picking' effect than he had been the night she had appeared back in his life. That moment after dealing with the motorbike accident victim when he'd noticed the slippers had replayed itself in his mind countless times since.

Knowing that Beth was living in the motel unit allo-

cated to new and single staff members had piqued his
curiosity, but *he* had been largely in control of any encounters they'd had so far. And he wanted to keep it that
way. He wasn't going to risk another put-down like the
one he'd received when he'd suggested they get together
for coffee.

Right now Beth was apparently hell-bent on reaching his home. His sanctuary.

It was too much!

He braked again, this time coming to a halt. He
pressed the button to unroll the window on the passenger side of the vehicle. Beth had seen him coming, of
course, and she actually looked eager to speak to him,
but Luke got in first.

'Where the hell do you think you're going?'

'Luke!' Beth's jaw dropped. 'I thought you were at
home.' She peered in at him, clearly disconcerted.
'There's a light on at your house.'

'It's automatic,' Luke snapped. 'To deter intruders.'

The rebuke went right over her head. 'I need a phone.
There's—'

'Hang on just a minute,' Luke ordered. 'How did you
know it was *my* house?'

'Ronald told me. No, Roz told me. Ronald just
showed me where it was, but that's not important, Luke.
There's a—'

'It might be important to me. Who the hell is Ronald
when he's at home?'

'For God's sake, Luke!' Beth raised her voice.
'There's a whole bunch of whales on your beach.'

'What?'

'I thought they were big rocks but then one of them
moved and I saw—'

'Get in.' Luke had started rolling downhill again even before Beth could shut her door properly. 'Have you reported it?'

'I didn't have my mobile with me. That's why I was going to the house. I mean, *your* house.'

Luke reached for the phone plugged into the Jeep's dashboard and punched in three numbers.

'Emergency services,' the voice responded promptly. 'What service do you require? Police, fire or ambulance?'

'Police.'

A new voice was on the line within seconds. 'What is your location?'

'Boulder Bay. Just north of Cloudy Bay, Marlborough.' Luke knew that the call was probably being answered in a major centre such as Wellington or Christchurch.

'And what is your emergency?'

'A mass whale stranding.' Luke could hear the surprised silence at the other end of the line as he concentrated on getting round a sharp bend in the road. 'Sorry, but this was the fastest way I could think of to activate a rescue operation. I don't have any numbers easily accessible for the Department of Conservation. They handle these sort of emergencies and we'll need some assistance pretty quickly.'

'Can you keep your mobile phone with you, sir?' The officer from the police communications centre had recovered from the surprise. 'We're onto it. Someone should contact you very soon.'

'Good. I should have some more information by then.' Having stopped the vehicle and killed the engine, Luke unhooked the phone and clipped it to his belt. 'Come on,' he said to Beth. 'We'd better go and have a closer look.'

Beth looked quite nervous about approaching the whales, but Luke had no hesitation in walking right up the nearest mammal. They were big, but not monstrous. Its blowhole was about level with Luke's waist and the whale was eight to ten feet long. Mostly black, there were large patches of white and the size of the fins was another good clue to their species.

'These are pilot whales,' he told Beth. 'That's good.'

'Is it?'

'If they were sperm whales there would be no rescue operation. They'd all have to be killed and buried.'

Beth was horrified. 'Why?'

'Because sperm whales have virtually no chance of survival once they're grounded like this.' Luke's head was turning rapidly, scanning the length of the small beach. 'It must have happened within the last hour or so. The tide's turned so we're going to have a long wait for enough water to try refloating them.' He shook his head. 'I'm amazed no one saw the pod coming in. There must be twenty or thirty animals here.'

Beth had come closer to the whale Luke was standing beside. She reached out a tentative hand and touched the rough cluster of barnacles that had seaweed trailing from it like an odd clump of hair. Then her hand stroked the black skin.

'It feels warm,' she said in surprise. 'But it's dry. Is it dead?'

'Hard to tell just by looking,' Luke said. 'They can hold their breath for an extraordinarily long time. They can go into a diving reflex when they're stranded like this.' He walked to the head of the whale and gently touched the edge of its eyeball. The eye and then the whole whale twitched.

'Watch out for the fluke.'

'The what?'

'The tail. It can swish pretty fast and it packs a punch.'

'Oh.' Beth hurriedly stepped away from the tail end of the large mammal.

'Don't step on the flippers!'

'OK.' Beth sounded out of her depth now and a second later she was clearly distressed. *'Oh!* Is that a baby?'

The whale she moved towards was only about the size of a large dolphin. It was lying on its side, a flipper moving weakly, and it made a mewling noise that had Beth dropping to a crouch beside it and reaching out to touch it.

'You poor wee thing. Luke?' Beth's face was upturned to him and her tone was beseeching. 'Can't we *do* something? Can we save it?'

'We'll certainly do our best.' How could he not respond to that heartfelt plea? The involvement of a baby in any kind of disaster exerted a greater tug on the heartstrings, but getting too emotionally involved with this kind of situation was a mistake that could easily affect the outcome. Luke turned away. 'Come up to the house. We need a whole heap of stuff.'

'Like what?'

'Blankets and sheets. Shovels. Buckets. We're going to have to keep them all cool and damp. We'll need to dig trenches to get any of them lying on their sides upright again. We also need to dig moats around their flippers and tails. This way.' Luke led Beth up the path that wound between boulders and into the native shrubbery that comprised his garden.

This was a bad idea, inviting Beth inside his home,

but what choice did he have? He couldn't carry everything himself and it could be some time before any further assistance arrived. The thought made Luke reach for his phone.

'Who are you calling? The police again?'

'No. My parents.' It was sad, the way a puzzled frown appeared on Beth's face. *Her* parents would probably be the last people she would think of contacting in any emergency. She had always had such a clear vision of the kind of family she wanted and it had come because she felt it had not been provided in her upbringing. The opposite had happened in Luke's case, but it had taken extreme circumstances to show him the value of what he had always had.

'They're involved with Project Jonah,' Luke explained. 'And they've had a lot of experience with whale rescues over the years. Hi, Mum— Hang on just a sec?'

Luke opened his front door and turned to Beth. 'There's a linen closet next to the bathroom. Get as many blankets and sheets as you can find. Take the ones off the bed as well.' He knew he sounded terse, but he couldn't help it.

Beth was going inside his house. It was never going to feel quite the same again, was it? He would think of her being there. Wondering what she thought about the things she saw. Whether she was drawn by the simplicity and homely feel of the place as much as he was. He would just be thinking of *her*, dammit, and he was already doing more than he should be of that.

'Mum? Are you still there? Listen, there's a pod of whales that's beached itself practically on my front doorstep…'

* * *

Luke's conversation with his mother faded as he went, presumably in the direction of a tool shed, and Beth went inside the house.

By the time she had taken a few steps she was feeling very puzzled. This must have been a holiday house in the past. Small and simply built, it had the feel of a quintessential New Zealand 'bach'. Modifications had been made in recent times, like the new kitchen and bathroom, but Luke choosing this as his home seemed inexplicable. It was so far removed from the kind of mansion he had aspired to as his career had been taking off. The kind of home her parents had owned.

Beth loved it. She could imagine how perfect a spot the small living area would be to watch the sun rise or set, but there was no time to stop and admire the sea view right now. The main bathroom was on the opposite side of the house, looking into a small garden, and the linen cupboard was easy to find.

Beth stacked all the sheets and blankets from the shelves near the front door and hesitated before fulfilling the other part of her instructions. She really didn't want to find Luke's bedroom and take the linen from his bed.

It was as difficult as she had anticipated. The bed *smelt* of Luke. Beth couldn't believe how she could have remembered that faint, musky scent that she associated so strongly with lazy early morning love-making or just lying in someone's arms, feeling loved and protected and so...*safe*.

She couldn't help glancing swiftly around to see if there was any evidence of a female resident. A comb or lipstick maybe, or a feminine robe hanging behind the door. The only evidence she found anywhere suggested that Luke's interest in housekeeping hadn't grown much since his days of sharing a house with other young doctors.

The aroma from the pile of dirty socks and underwear in the corner of the new-looking *en suite* bathroom did not evoke any poignant memories. Beth's nose crinkled and she hurried outside with the first armload of linen. Going back for the rest, she noted the dirty dishes on the kitchen bench and the CDs scattered on the floor of the living area.

The cover of the uppermost disc caught her eye. *Seventies Retro* it was called and it brought back a sudden and unwanted memory of the fancy-dress party of that era that she had attended with Luke to celebrate the thirtieth birthday of one of the surgical registrars he lived with. Beth had gone dressed in an orange Paisley caftan she had found in a vintage clothing store and she had covered her black curls with a long blonde wig.

She'd had the *best* time. The only really good time she had ever had attending the kind of parties Luke had preferred. Maybe that had been because the elite of the local medical community had all been in disguise that night, letting their hair down and having too much fun to be concerned with flaunting position or wealth or superiority.

And she had gone home with Luke well before the others had left the party venue and Luke had slowly removed her wig and that caftan and had looked at her with *that* look and said softly, 'I just *love* unwrapping presents!'

But it had been Beth who had received the gift that night. Love-making so intense but so gentle. Until Beth had demanded more and had been given a lot more than she had bargained for. A lesson, in fact, on just how wild sex could be with a partner you trusted completely.

She had never trusted anyone else that completely,

but that was only to be expected, wasn't it? Luke had been her first real love and she had given him her heart. Maybe he still had a piece or two of it. Or perhaps she had lost them when she'd tried to put her life back together. It would explain why she'd never been able to offer anyone else the kind of love and commitment she had felt for Luke.

Could anything else ever be that good again?

It was a relief to leave the house and the memory behind. Luke was on the path with a laden wheelbarrow and her first armload of linen was balanced precariously on top of buckets and tools.

'Help's on its way,' Luke informed her briskly. 'A Department of Conservation team is flying in from Wellington and Mum and Dad are rounding up local volunteers. The police are going to cordon off the road so we don't get inundated with sightseers, and I've offered the house as a base for the operations manager. They'll need kitchen facilities and so on.'

'You sound like you know all about this kind of thing.'

'Not really. I helped at a stranding years ago on Farewell Spit, which is a much more common place for this to happen. I would have thought Boulder Bay beach was too steep and rocky, but there you go. It's happened.'

'They do it when one of them gets sick or injured, don't they?' Beth stumbled a little as she followed Luke. At 9 p.m. it still wasn't completely dark but it was hard to see her feet around the pile of blankets she held.

'Sometimes it's because the leader is sick or disorientated and sometimes they just don't know why it happens. There'll be people coming to study the scene.

They make a site map and examine and take samples from any dead whales.' Luke looked up as a set of car headlights appeared on the road winding down the hillside.

'I hope that's my parents,' he said. 'I've asked Dad to ferry other volunteers down from the top of the hill. We don't want too many vehicles down here or there won't be room for the heavy stuff.'

'Heavy stuff?'

'Tractors. Boats. Generators for the lights, that sort of thing.'

'Good grief! I had no idea how much was involved in rescuing whales.'

'Are you working tonight?'

'No. And I've got the day off tomorrow.'

'Good.' Luke smiled. 'How about coming to help me with a spot of triage, then, Nurse?'

'Certainly, Doctor.' Beth smiled back. 'Do you have some colour-coded triage cards in that wheelbarrow first-aid kit of yours?'

'No, but I've got a can of spray paint. We'll put a big "X" on any obviously dead whales and that will save time later.'

The feeling of excited anticipation that the prospect of working with Luke was engendering evaporated. Beth didn't want any of these whales to be dead. This was an extraordinary experience to be thrown into and Beth's connection suddenly went way past being the person to have discovered the emergency.

She wasn't about to stop and try to analyse why it was so important to her. Maybe it was because the whales had chosen Luke's beach to strand themselves on. Or maybe she had accorded the situation the status of an omen regarding her new life in this place.

It didn't matter. Her determination to succeed was powerful enough to feel like desperation and there was no time to lose.

At least fifty volunteers had gathered within an hour, and until the Department of Conservation officials arrived it was Luke's parents, Don and Barbara, who took charge of the rescue operation. One whale was already dead—possibly the sick or injured member of the pod that had prompted the rest to strand themselves.

Pairs and trios of people were assigned a now numbered whale each to care for. Beth waited until finally Barbara shone her torch on the piece of paper she was writing on and then looked up.

'Beth Dawson?'

'I'm here.'

'We'll get you to look after the baby. Jack—you can help. You've got some experience.'

Jack showed Beth how to gouge a shallow trench in the sand parallel to the tiny whale's body. Luke came past just as they were completing this first task.

'That looks deep enough. Let's try getting him upright. Dad?' Luke's father was talking to a man as he shone a torch on one of the larger whales. 'Could you give us a hand?'

Don was also satisfied with the trench digging. 'Make sure you keep his flippers flat against the body when we roll him,' he advised. 'They're easy to injure.'

The four of them managed to roll the baby whale from its side quite easily, and the trench looked as though it would keep him upright securely.

'Do you know about making a moat around the flippers and tail?' Don asked Beth.

She nodded. 'And Jack said we can't make it too deep because that might make it difficult to shift him later.'

'Sorry, Dad.' Luke was draping a folded sheet over the whale's body behind the blowhole. 'You know Jack, don't you? This is Beth Dawson.'

'Hello, there.' Don Savage had a smile identical to his son's, and Beth found herself smiling back just as enthusiastically at the wiry man who looked to be in his seventies. 'That name sounds familiar.' He peered at her more closely. 'You're not *the* Beth, by any chance, are you?'

'Um…' Beth had no idea what she could say to that. What did he mean? Had Luke been bitter enough to describe her in lurid detail to his parents perhaps?

'Your mate, Pete, is just over here.' Luke took his father's elbow and steered him away without acknowledging the interchange. 'He and Doris are looking after number fifteen. You might like to come and check out their moats.'

Doris was the woman from the dairy and Beth had been astonished at how good it was to see a familiar face amongst the volunteers. A not-so-pleasant surprise came when she saw the arrival of the pretty blonde woman she had seen Luke talking to that day. At least she was directed well away from Beth's position to join the group caring for the large bull whale who was assumed to be the pod leader.

Jack, Beth's only partner in caring for the baby whale, was a man in his fifties and he was rapidly becoming a friend.

'You're going to be OK, Willy,' he told their whale.

Beth grinned. 'Willy? As in *Free Willy*?'

'Yup. It's the only whale name I know. Unless you can think up a better one?'

'Willy's fine by me.'

Naming the baby made it all seem even more personal. Beth joined people queuing to share buckets and make trips into the surf and back, carrying water to fill the moats and tip carefully over the whales' backs. Beth knew without being told not to tip water into Willy's blowhole but she hadn't known it still needed to stay moist. Using a corner of the wet sheet to dampen the skin on the whale's head, Beth leapt back and nearly fell over when it released a breath with a noise like the vent being opened on a pressure cooker.

She laughed, but the spray was cold. Her legs were now soaked from the knees down from filling the bucket in the surf, and it all got colder over the next hour or two. The first of a supply of hot drinks was provided at the same time as the generators were set up to flood the area with artificial light, and the atmosphere changed as the rescue operation went into another gear under the expert supervision of Department of Conservation experts.

No one was more determined or focussed than Beth, however.

'I think number fifteen must be Willy's mother,' she told Jack excitedly. 'Have you noticed how she answers every time he makes a sound?'

Number fifteen didn't just respond vocally to the baby. It had a tendency to thrash its tail, which had Doris and Pete scrambling out of the way at regular intervals. The operations manager became concerned.

'We might have to try moving the baby. You're kind of hemmed in here and it could be dangerous if this one gets any more distressed.'

'But we think that's Willy's mother,' Beth exclaimed. 'If we separate them, she'll only get more upset, won't she?'

'*Willy?*' The Department of Conservation official shook his head, clearly unimpressed with Beth's bond with the baby whale. 'We'll see how it goes,' he said noncommittally. 'I'll be back.'

Jack took a turn hauling buckets of water just after 1 a.m. 'The tide's turned,' he told Beth. 'It's on its way back in.'

'How deep does it need to get before we start refloating the whales?'

'We'll be about knee deep by the time the adults can be shifted. We'll have to hang onto this little chap for a while, though, or even shift him further up the beach. Once we get them all back into the water we have to keep them together in a group for an least an hour to try and reorientate them.'

'Is that so they won't just beach themselves again?'

'That's right. And after we've let them go, we'll all have to stand in a line in the waves and bang metal things together to try and persuade them to head out to sea. We're in for the long haul, I'm afraid. You're not too tired or cold yet, are you?'

'No.' Beth's tone was valiant but she *was* tired. And very cold. And her stomach was hurting. When the next cup of soup came her way she found she couldn't swallow more than half of it. The warmth was welcome but it made her feel sick.

Cramp, she decided, from crouching over Willy too long without stretching her muscles.

'I'll get some more water,' she told Jack. 'Be back in a minute.'

Luke saw Beth struggling to carry a full bucket of sea water.

She looked exhausted. And very pale. Luke couldn't suppress the memory of how much he'd always loved the smooth, milky quality of Beth's skin, but seeing her right now did not make him want her the way it had in the swimming pool the other day.

What it did make him want to do was to take her in his arms and hold her until she warmed up. Until the lines of strain on her face eased. He wanted to tell her what a great job she was doing and how impressed he was at the way she threw herself so wholeheartedly into helping others—people or animals. He wanted to tell her that everything was going to be all right. She didn't have to be so worried.

The only comfort he could offer, however, was a smile and an outstretched hand to relieve her of the burden of the heavy bucket.

'Here, let me help you with that. You look done in.'

Beth hesitated, as though she was about to refuse his assistance. She gave in and let him take the bucket but she didn't return his smile. She grimaced, in fact, and dug the fingers of her right hand into her abdomen just beside her hip.

'I'm OK,' she said. 'I've just got a stitch from carrying that bucket.'

'Have a rest for a minute.'

'Mmm.' Beth looked away abruptly. Had she read a

level of concern she didn't appreciate? Luke carefully made his expression and tone as neutral as possible.

'I'll bet you're wishing you hadn't come to live in Hereford after all.'

A startled glance let him know he'd said the wrong thing…again.

'I meant this,' he added quickly. 'There's not many places you could go to and end up having to knock yourself out saving whales.'

'No.' Beth sounded incredibly weary. Was she thinking of other reasons why she might wish she hadn't come to live in Hereford? Like seeing him again?

The mournful cry of a nearby whale seemed to echo Luke's melancholy thought. He stared at the back of Beth's head for a second as she started walking slowly back towards her own whale. Then he followed.

'Why *did* you come here, Beth?'

'I told you. I wanted a new start.'

'But why *here*? In Hereford.'

Beth shrugged. 'The job just happened to be in the nursing gazette. I'd been out to the airport to say goodbye to a friend and I guess the time was right to make a decision. I didn't want to do anything as drastic as Neroli had done, though, like leaving nursing. Or New Zealand.'

'Neroli? Your friend with the red hair and freckles? The one that always laughed a lot?'

'That's her.' Beth turned and smiled, as though pleased that Luke had remembered so clearly. 'She hadn't been laughing much in the last few months she was here, though.'

'Why not?'

'She got held at knife point in ED by a gang member who was as high as a kite on drugs. It was terrifying enough to make her throw in the towel and give up nursing. I can't say I blame her either. It *was* pretty scary.'

Luke caught his breath. 'Were you *there* when it happened?'

'Yes.'

And she'd been caught in the middle of a gang war on her first night at Ocean View. She must have been as terrified as Neroli had been and yet she'd defended herself without hesitation. More than that—she'd set the tone for the whole department to cope with a nasty few hours.

A peculiar sensation sneaked up on Luke. It wasn't that Beth had changed into some stroppy individual who went around sorting out anybody who displeased her. She had always been amazing. Brave and clever. She wouldn't attack anyone without justification.

He'd never understood why she'd wanted so little to do with her family until her bitter remarks in the car park that morning.

He'd never understood quite why she'd dumped him either, but the thought that she might have been justified was not one he wanted to explore. He'd been put down enough by Beth, and this wasn't the time to go looking for any more emotional injuries. Besides, she'd made it quite clear that she didn't want to start raking up the past.

'What?' Beth had turned again and was looking at him oddly.

Luke blinked. 'What?' he echoed.

'You just muttered something about raking up the past.'

'Did I?' Luke tried to dismiss the embarrassment of having spoken that last thought aloud. 'Maybe that's what *I* was doing when I came back here.'

Beth gave him a sharp look. 'I had no idea *you* were living here.'

Her tone implied that it was the last place she would have come if she *had* known. Luke gritted his teeth. And he'd been trying to avoid a put-down, too.

'This is the last place I would have expected you to be,' Beth continued. 'You told me you grew up in Nelson.'

'I went to school in Nelson,' Luke corrected.

'And you called that Hicksville. I seem to remember you saying you wouldn't be caught dead, trying to practise any kind of medicine in some provincial backwater.'

Luke's shrug dismissed the comment as irrelevant now. 'Things change. People change.'

Not that much they didn't. Beth took the last few steps towards Willy in silence.

Things didn't change to that kind of degree unless something absolutely catastrophic happened. The new chill that suddenly ran through Beth was enough to make her shudder.

Was Luke sick? Had all the stress of his ambition and workload and then his sister dying given him a heart attack at an early age, maybe, and forced him to slow down?

The fear the thought provoked was powerful enough to make Beth realise just how much she had been kidding herself.

She had never stopped loving Luke Savage.

She never would.

Turning back, Beth searched his face but she could find no answers.

'What changed, Luke?' she asked quietly. 'Why *are* you living here?'

'It's home.'

The simple words explained nothing and yet they explained it all.

It was precisely what Beth was searching for, wasn't it? But home could be a person as much as a place. And the home that Beth's soul craved had nothing to do with any real estate or stupid casserole dishes.

Her home could only be with the man she loved.

A man who no longer loved her.

She was still staring at Luke when she heard someone call his name with some urgency from near the car park.

And Luke, with a smile that seemed almost apologetic, handed the bucket back to Beth.

Then he turned and walked away.

CHAPTER SIX

WHY had he been embarrassed to admit that Hereford was home?

The only place Luke wanted to be. Would Beth see him as a failure, having traded his dreams of fame and fortune to be a simple country doctor? Living in a place small enough to ensure he was recognised wherever he went? Being on call every second night and quite likely to have some member of the community stop him in the supermarket to ask advice about some minor ailment?

And did it really matter what Beth thought of him?

Yes and no.

Luke smiled at the man waiting beside his Jeep, whose injury someone had alerted him to.

'What's happened, mate?'

'I fell over my bloody shovel,' the man growled.

'Let's have a look.' Luke shone his torch onto the man's shin. 'You're going to need a couple of stitches in that, I'm afraid,' he said seconds later. 'You might need a tetanus booster as well if that shovel was rusty. I'll put a dressing on it and someone will be able to run you down to the hospital.'

'Can it wait? The tide's turning. I wouldn't want to miss refloating these guys. Not when we've worked this hard already.'

Yeah. Some things were worth putting up with a bit of discomfort for, weren't they? Luke did his best to make sure the owner of the leg wound wouldn't suffer from waiting for a while. He cleaned the wound and covered it with a sterile dressing and then bandaged it carefully. He even scored a plastic bag from the team manning the barbecues and taped it securely over the bandage to keep it dry.

'Make sure you get into the emergency department as soon as you can,' he warned. 'This isn't going to hold it together for that long and I'd hate you to end up with an infection.'

He watched the determination with which his patient headed back towards the whales. They were reaching the low point of this rescue operation. It was an ordeal to hang in there and keep going. Some people had given in and gone home for a rest.

Beth wasn't one of them. Luke found his gaze wandering as he searched for the small shape of the baby whale and its carers.

Of course it mattered what Beth thought of him. He'd lost so much in his life already. He was about to lose even more, with his best mate only having such a short time left. The sadness that clouded Luke's life could easily shift to encompass what he'd lost with Beth and override any lasting bitterness.

The bitterness had only lasted this long because he'd never understood quite why it had gone so wrong. Sure, they'd started having arguments. Silly arguments over things like which restaurant he'd chosen to take

Beth out to or the wine he'd chosen to accompany the dinner.

Nothing he'd done had seemed to be right and, yes, it had got his back up. When the disagreements had started on important things like his friends and his career, of course he'd had to take a stand. And, of course, he had started spending longer and longer hours at work. Why go home when time with your partner made you feel you just weren't good enough?

It hadn't been anything like that to start with, though, had it? Time together had been so precious. He had loved everything about Beth. Just being with her. Talking to her. Listening to her. *Touching* her.

Oh...*God*!

Luke shoved the last of his supplies back into his first-aid kit and zipped the pack shut.

Why *had* it gone so terribly wrong?

He hadn't deserved to be dumped but sadness still outweighed anger. Maybe if he could understand what had happened he might be able to move on and be confident that he didn't make the same mistakes in a future relationship.

What if Beth decided to stay in Hereford and they spent years avoiding really talking to each other because he was too proud to ask what he'd done that had been so wrong?

If they spent years missing out on a potential friendship because of his pride?

Luke was all too aware of just how precious friends were.

He pushed the first-aid kit into the back of the Jeep. The next opportunity he got, he was going to talk to Beth, dammit.

Really talk.

* * *

It was all becoming an ordeal.

A second adult whale died and a whisper of gloom spread along Boulder Bay beach. The waves crept a little further up the sand each time they rolled in and as they got closer, the chill increased. Jack seemed as miserable as Beth was now feeling and for some time now he had said almost nothing. They crouched on either side of the baby whale, scooping water from the moats around his flippers and tail to splash over the sodden sheet covering his back.

Beth was on autopilot, trying to ignore her wet jeans, the cold gritty sand in her shoes and the irritating pain in her side that wouldn't go away. She just needed to distract herself enough to hang on and see this through. Another half-hour or so and the waves would be covering her feet, and by then they should have started to refloat the first of the mammals.

The best method to distract herself was to watch what was happening in the circles of light away from her own, but the way her gaze invariably found Luke in the crowd of people only added to her despondency.

He was moving between the groups. Administering first aid when needed, but more often he was just talking to people. Encouraging them. Helping. Beth saw him touch someone's arm, pat someone else on the back and once he was enfolded in an enthusiastic hug from a very large and very short woman.

What became even more noticeable than the physical connection he constantly made with these people was the effect his presence clearly had. Women and men smiled when they saw him approaching and the only laughter to be heard on the beach now was always close to where Luke was.

This *was* his home, wasn't it? These were *his* people. Beth wanted to be a part of the community that Luke cared about so much.

No. If she was honest, she wanted to be singled out as special. She wanted to be the one person Luke cared for more than anyone else.

The way she cared about him.

And it could never happen. Beth had made sure of that, hadn't she, by ending their relationship in the first place? At the time it had seemed like she'd had absolutely no choice. But now, with the changes she saw in Luke—even if she didn't understand how they had happened—it felt like she had made a huge mistake.

Beth's spirits slipped another notch and when she heard Jack groan it seemed as though he was reading her mind. But that was ridiculous.

'Are you all right, Jack?'

'I've got a bit of a pain.'

'Whereabouts?'

'In my chest. It's OK, I've got my spray somewhere.'

Beth's knees protested as she straightened and the cramp in her abdomen tightened, but she was well distracted from her own discomfort.

'Is it angina? Do you have a heart condition, Jack?'

'Yeah…kind of. Nothing too serious.'

'You've never had a heart attack?'

'No.'

'How bad is this pain now? Is it the same as your usual angina?'

'It's just kind of gripping me.'

'Whereabouts exactly?' Beth had come around

Willy's head and didn't even notice the spray from his blowhole wetting her hair as she saw Jack's clenched fist against the centre of his chest. 'Is it just in your chest?'

'Goes down my arm a bit, too.'

'Where's your spray?'

'In my pocket, I think.' Jack fumbled with the zip on his jacket. 'Damn it, my hands are so cold they won't work properly.'

'Here, let me.' Beth unzipped the jacket. The small cylinder of GTN spray was easy to find in Jack's back pocket. 'Lift your tongue up,' she directed Jack. Then she sprayed two squirts of the medication. 'You sit down for a minute and rest.'

Beth felt his pulse, which seemed quite steady and strong, but she was alarmed, nonetheless. Even if the pain went away with rest and medication, Jack needed a check-up to determine whether this was angina or a heart attack. And he certainly shouldn't be standing around in the cold, let alone planning to battle the surf to help refloat the whales.

Beth wasn't surprised that Luke noticed what was going on. He was beside them less than a minute after Jack had sat down on the sand.

'What's going on?'

'Jack's got some angina. He's just used his spray.'

'Has that helped, Jack?'

'Not yet. Maybe I should have some more.'

'How are you feeling otherwise?'

'Cold. A bit sick, I guess.'

'Right. We're going to send you into Ocean View to

get checked. I'll get a stretcher and we'll get you up to the ambulance at the top of the hill.'

'Don't be daft. I can walk.' Jack glared at Luke. 'There's no way I'm getting carried off this beach in front of all these people.'

'Hmm. How bad is this pain at the moment, Jack? On a scale of one to ten with ten, being the worst.'

'Two.'

Luke chuckled. 'You wouldn't be lying, would you, Jack?'

'I'm not getting carried.'

'Fine. We'll walk as far as the car park. But you'll let me support you and we'll walk very slowly.'

Beth scrambled to her feet again. 'I can help.'

Luke shook his head. 'Look after your whale. I'll find someone to come and take Jack's place for you.'

But it was Luke who came back to her a little while later.

'He looks OK,' he told Beth. 'Another dose of GTN and some oxygen fixed the pain, but I've sent him in for an ECG anyway.' He stooped to collect a half-bucket of water from the moat Beth had just refilled and dribbled it over Willy's back. 'There's no one free to help you just now so I'll stay unless I'm needed somewhere else.'

'Thanks.' Beth could think of nothing else to say and there wasn't much point in dreaming up a conversation, was there? It probably wouldn't be long before someone else wanted Luke's attention.

The silence was awkward and it was Luke who broke it.

'I'm glad you came to Hereford, Beth.'

'Really?' Beth couldn't help sounding surprised.

'That wasn't the impression *I* got. You looked horrified when you saw me in ED.'

'I *was* surprised,' Luke conceded. 'For a second I thought I was seeing a ghost.'

He smiled at Beth as he put the bucket down. Surely it was a trick of the artificial light that made the smile seem to wobble so precariously? But then Luke dipped his head, adding to the impression that something had saddened him immeasurably. He cleared his throat and the new cheeriness in his tone was definitely forced.

'So…what do you think of Hereford so far, anyway?'

'I love it.'

'Yeah? It *is* a great place.'

'I even went out yesterday to look at a couple of houses for sale.'

'No kidding?' Luke almost sounded pleased at the idea that Beth was planning to stay. She smiled and nodded as she stretched out her hand.

'Can I have that bucket? I'll go and get some more water.'

It wasn't far to go to fill the bucket now. A wave broke over Beth's feet and the icy foam reached to her knees. She was shivering by the time she arrived back beside Willy.

'What's he doing?'

'What, that sort of hiccupping? Wasn't he doing that before?'

'No. He's never made a noise like that.' Beth put the bucket down and crouched to peer at the whale's face. 'Are you all right, Willy?'

'Willy?'

'Jack named him.' Beth sighed. 'I hope he's going to be all right.'

'Who? Jack or Willy?

'Both of them.'

The new silence was quite long enough for Beth to fret about Willy's condition. He probably still needed his mother to feed him. How long would he last without milk? He'd hardly moved for the last hour or more, come to think of it. Maybe one of the Department of Conservation officials would know enough about whales to be able to reassure her. Beth looked up to see if she could spot someone in one of the bright reflecting vests, but all she managed to do was catch sight of the blonde walking away from her group towards the car-parking area. Looking for Luke perhaps?

Beth's gaze automatically shifted. 'Friend of yours, isn't she?'

Luke turned his head swiftly. 'That's Maree.' He nodded. 'Yes, she's a good friend. She's also the sister of my ex-brother-in-law.'

Beth's heart sank like a stone. 'So you *did* get married, then?'

'No, of course I didn't. What on earth makes you say that?'

Beth's mouth opened and then closed again. Why had he said 'of course'? Surely he couldn't mean that if he hadn't married *her* he wouldn't want to marry anyone else. That was ridiculous.

But it *had* sounded like that, hadn't it?

Luke saw her expression and completely misread it. 'Oh...right. In-laws can get complicated, I guess. Maree's brother was married to my sister.' He looked away from Beth. 'I never got married.'

'Why not?' The personal question popped out before Beth even thought of preventing it.

'Never met the right person, I guess.'

'Not for lack of trying, though.' Beth's smile was wry.

'What?'

'You had a different woman on your arm every time I saw you after we broke up, Luke. Right up until you moved to Wellington.'

Even in the shadows Beth could see the way Luke's face tightened angrily. He started pulling back the covering over Willy, which was starting to slip, with jerky movements.

'What did you expect me to do when you cut me out of your life, Beth? Sit and mope? Turn into a monk?'

He seemed to collect himself. 'I was angry,' he said more quietly. 'Angry enough to try and prove that there were women out there who actually thought I *was* good enough for them.'

A wave reached as far as Beth was crouching and the icy water soaked the seat of her jeans. She stood up hurriedly.

'I never thought you weren't good enough, Luke.'

'That was the impression I certainly got.'

Beth had to stoop suddenly to catch the bucket the retreating wave was stealing. The pain in her side grabbed at her but she shook her head, denying the pain as well as Luke's impression.

'We were just too different, that's all. Our values were too different.'

'But we never disagreed about important things like values. We argued about silly things. Like that car I wanted to buy.'

'The BMW?'

'Yeah. What *was* so wrong with that?'

'I told you at the time. I didn't like that it was such a status symbol.'

'It was a good, safe car. That was the reason I wanted it. To keep us safe. To keep *you* safe.'

'So you said.' Beth hated the way she was sounding. She didn't want to argue with Luke. She didn't want to go over such old ground like this. She was cold, tired and miserable, and there still didn't seem to be an end in sight to this ordeal.

'You hated my friends, too.'

Make that both ordeals. The whale rescue *and* Luke's dissection of their break-up.

'Some of them were snobs,' Beth said wearily. 'If you weren't climbing the same social ladder they were, you weren't worth talking to. You fitted *right* in. I had no desire to be part of that set.'

'Then why the hell did you go out with a doctor in the first place?'

'I…I fell in love with you, that's why.' The words almost choked Beth. 'I thought you might be different. A country boy who had worked very hard to get qualified. Someone who came from a background very different from mine. From a *real* family. I thought you might feel the same about the things that really matter.'

'Such as?'

Beth reached out to stroke Willy. 'What I was just talking about,' she said quietly. 'Family.'

Luke groaned. 'Oh, come on! I value my family a hell of lot more than you value yours. I had to practically force you to introduce me. It was months before you would and they only lived across town, and when you did…'

Someone said hello to Luke as they passed and someone else was shouting something about getting ropes to get the first whales ready for shifting, but Luke seemed to hear nothing but his own thoughts. When he spoke again after that pause, he sounded almost bewildered.

'When you did finally take me to meet your parents—that was when things started to go so wrong between us, wasn't it?'

Beth couldn't deny it. Not that she got the chance.

'I'd set out to try and impress your parents for your sake but it backfired on me, didn't it? That was when you decided I wasn't up to scratch. Everything I did was somehow wrong after that. Even my career. You actually tried to talk me out of applying for the job I'd dreamed of getting.'

'And you applied for it anyway.'

They were at the crux of it all now. The final showdown. Beth was surprised to find so much of her anger still there.

That anger had been why she had refused to consider going to Wellington with Luke. That job had represented every doubt she had been having about their future together. When he'd gone ahead and applied for it without even telling her, all those doubts had seemed justified and his determination to accept the position if it had been offered had been what had finally split them irrevocably.

Beth had had the torment of hearing about his successful interviews from others and then watching him work out his notice in Auckland with the air of being about to move onto something much better.

'Of course I did.' Luke was still sounding bewildered. 'I couldn't understand why you were so against it. It was an astonishing position for anyone at my stage to even be considered for.'

'And you wouldn't have got that far if my father hadn't been so impressed by you.'

Luke shook his head. 'I got the job on my own merits. Sure, the director of cardiac surgery in Wellington was an old friend of your father's—'

'His *closest* friend,' Beth cut in.

Luke ignored the interruption. 'And maybe it helped my application get a second glance, but I competed on an even field with a lot of other applicants after that— applicants from all over the world, no less. I deserved that job, Beth. I *earned* it.'

'Of course you did.'

'And what the hell was so wrong with wanting to succeed? I would have had to have changed my entire career and lifestyle to make you happy then. Of course I wasn't going to do that. For anyone. You were right. I was a country boy and I *had* worked bloody hard to get where I was.'

He'd done it now, though, hadn't he? Made a complete U-turn in his career and his lifestyle. Beth wanted so badly to ask why but Luke wanted an answer to his own question. And he deserved one because he seemed genuinely puzzled.

Did Luke really have cause to look back and see her as being critical and destructive without adequate reason? If he did, it wasn't entirely her fault. She'd tried to explain but she herself hadn't really understood how crucial what had been missing from her own life had been. Her objections could have come across as being an inverted snobbery, but Luke hadn't been willing to listen hard enough, had he? He'd overridden her objections with increasing impatience until that last, dreadful fight about the job he had intended to compete for.

She had been right to take her own stand then, hadn't she? Or had fear warped her perspective?

Beth could see the operations manager walking towards them but Luke was still clearly waiting for an answer.

'Nothing,' she said finally. 'There's nothing wrong with wanting to succeed.'

'So what was it, then, Beth?' Luke's tone was despairing. 'What did I actually *do* that was so wrong?'

Luke's face seemed to have captured and condensed that whisper of gloom that had been doing the rounds of Boulder Bay beach and the sadness Beth could see brought tears to her eyes.

She bit her lip and dropped her gaze. 'I was scared,' she admitted.

'Scared of what?'

Beth was unwilling to raise her face and look at Luke, but his gentle touch under her chin made hiding impossible.

'What were you so scared of, Beth?'

'That…that I'd chosen someone who was going to end up being just like my father.'

The operations manager was beside Willy now. He looked from Beth to Luke and frowned.

'Not interrupting something, am I?'

'No.' Luke's shoulders slumped a little as he turned away from Beth. 'What's up, Jim? Nobody's injured, are they?'

'No. We've got enough water to start refloating. We're probably more likely to get injuries now than at any other time, so I just wanted to make sure you knew what was happening.'

'I'll come with you.'

Beth watched the two men walk away. Dawn was breaking finally and she could see beyond the pools of artificial light. She could see the rescuers with the whales closer to the water, waves breaking above their knees and the foam up past their waists. They were hanging onto their charges and seemed to be rocking them in the water. It was only now that Beth realised how the noise level had grown as instructions were shouted. Her conversation with Luke had been so intense she had been unaware of the shift into the next phase of the rescue effort.

She wasn't sure she was ready for this. Already physically challenged, that time with Luke had exhausted her emotionally. Had she ever really tried to look at things from Luke's perspective? No wonder he was bitter.

'It's hopeless,' she said aloud. 'Isn't it, Willy?'

The sound from Willy was loud. Louder than any he'd made for hours. The answering cry from whale number fifteen was even louder. Willy wriggled and the ankle deep water was enough to let him move.

'Oh!' Beth grabbed the baby whale behind his fin. 'Don't move yet, Willy. It's all right. Everything's going to be all right.'

Someone Beth didn't know came to help her hold onto Willy, and things seemed to start moving a lot faster on the beach from that point.

A tractor and ropes were being used to move whales into deeper water and the sand and surf boiled with the movement of their huge tails. Beth did as she was told and struggled to keep her footing in the icy water and keep Willy upright and prevent his blowhole being swamped as each new wave surged in. Everywhere people were shouting and moving. Some even swam beside their whales.

And everywhere Beth found herself watching for Luke, but she couldn't find him and somehow that seemed perfectly appropriate.

Luke was gone and there was really no point in dwelling on how much either of them had been to blame for what had happened in the past.

The next wave actually lifted Beth from her feet and Willy moved away from her to tuck himself alongside whale number fifteen.

'Come away,' Beth's new partner told her. 'Don't try and get between them. Look—they're moving.'

All the whales were moving now. They slipped into deeper water and gathered into a single group. Beth joined in the loud cheer that ran through the crowd. Surf splashed her face and mingled with tears that were flowing freely.

Maybe it was finally over.

CHAPTER SEVEN

THE noise was deafening.

Clanging of metal against metal. People shouting. Outboard motors on inflatable boats revving as they patrolled the sea between the human wall and the pod of pilot whales now milling about in deep water. A helicopter overhead with cameras taking footage for a television news broadcast because it was finally light enough to see what was happening clearly.

It would have taken many more decibels, however, to silence the words Luke could hear in his head.

No wonder Beth had run from their relationship.

Luke had never denied being ambitious. He'd even recognised it as being a stumbling block in his relationship with Beth when they'd started arguing about that job in Wellington. Right now he could also see it as arrogance.

His refusal to contemplate compromise had seemed perfectly justifiable at the time. He would have been doing it for them both. His wife—and, eventually, his children—could only have benefited from his success and the more money and power and prestige he could have garnered, the better off they would all have been.

Those ambitions were long gone, of course. Jodie's

illness and death had pulled an emotional rug from beneath Luke with enough of a jerk to send them flying. There was no way Beth could be afraid of him evolving into a clone of her father now, surely?

Or was there?

She'd been scared.

Why hadn't he seen that? Of course she'd been scared. But, then, Beth had always been a little nervous of anything new in those days. She'd always tried so hard to get things right and her self-esteem had never been as high as it should have been. And no wonder. How much of her life had she spent trying to win a little attention from her parents?

What had she said? That the only thing she'd ever done that they'd really approved of had been to produce him as a potential son-in-law?

Luke couldn't imagine what it would be like, growing up in an atmosphere where acceptance and love were scarce commodities.

If he'd been thinking about her, rather than the impression he'd been trying to make that night she'd taken him home to meet her parents, he might have recognised her reticence as fear then, too.

She'd been so quiet. Self-effacing. Listening to praise of her siblings with apparent interest. Simply smiling at what Luke had seen as fond teasing about her own choices.

'Beth could have managed medical school, you know, Luke,' Nigel Dawson had said. 'She's bright enough.'

'Just stubborn,' Celia Dawson had added. 'Do you know, Luke, when she was a toddler, she would wear her shoes on the wrong feet all day, rather than admit she'd got it wrong?'

And Nigel had laughed. 'Must have hurt her feet. Maybe she's not so bright after all!'

Luke had winked at Beth to let her know he'd known it hadn't been serious. That he had been laughing with her father, not at *her*. And even then, Luke realised with shame, he would have been flattered at the idea that he would become a man like Nigel Dawson.

Who hadn't heard of the famous surgeon? The man was an arrogant bastard, sure, but everybody knew he was the best. He had a terrible temper and was renowned for throwing things in the OR. He treated his wife, who was invariably his anaesthetist with contempt in the professional arena but he was a brilliant surgeon. The best.

And Luke had been hungry to be the best.

He wouldn't have been anything like Beth's father in any other respect, though. The very thought was shocking.

As shocking as suddenly being underwater when he stepped forward into a hole and found himself out of his depth. He surfaced a second or two later, swimming back to waist-deep water, but he'd lost one of the iron rods he had been striking against each other so there seemed little point in staying where he was.

They would all soon go back to the beach in any case, leaving the boats to patrol the bay and hopefully keep the whales from stranding themselves again. A huge driftwood bonfire had been built so that the volunteers could dry off and warm themselves, and he could smell the sausages and bacon being cooked up for a celebratory breakfast on the gas barbecues. After the long, hard night, a celebration was called for.

But Luke had never felt less like celebrating.

Any anger he'd directed towards Beth for the last few

years had suddenly done a neat U-turn and was now directed at himself.

He hadn't had any inkling of Beth's real fear, had he? And he hadn't given an inch. He'd taken all her initially gentle objections as personal criticism and had fought back. He'd even dismissed having it pointed out that their dreams might be taking them in different directions and that could ultimately destroy what they had together. If Beth wanted to be with him, her dreams could just be modified, couldn't they? They would do it his way or they wouldn't do it at all. He'd shouted at her that night. He'd walked away.

He hadn't been so very different from her father at all, really. And if he'd kept going in the same direction, he *would* have ended up being a clone of a man Beth had done her best to avoid claiming any connection with.

Luke had brought his loneliness on himself and in some ways he should thank Beth for kicking him out of her life. If he'd had Beth with him during those grim times with Jodie he would have used that calm strength she had when on familiar territory. Depending on that could have blocked him from learning what he had needed to learn.

What Beth had always known.

Luke paused as he walked clear of the surf. He'd fallen in love with this place because being here had given him peace at a time he'd needed it badly. Now that he was thinking so clearly, he could recognise that peace as an echo of what he'd found with Beth all those years ago.

What he'd lost.

What he would give anything to get back.

He'd lost Beth because of who he had been becoming, but that person bore no relation to the person Luke really was. The person he was now being true to. If Beth knew how much he'd changed—*really* changed—would that make things any different?

Luke badly wanted things to be different.

If nothing else, he had to apologise. Properly. Maybe Beth would be able to forgive him and a friendship might be possible.

Something more than friendship was too big an ask to even contemplate right now, and it would certainly remain an impossibility if the past couldn't be put to rest. Luke had to find Beth. He had to see if she might be at least willing to talk to him.

Volunteers were returning to the beach now but Luke actually waded back into the water as he searched for Beth. The general mood of the crowd was jubilant and Luke could hear laughter and good-natured ribbing as people compared their injuries or discomforts.

'I'm frozen! My hands are blue!'

'I'm *so* tired, I can hardly stand up!'

'I'm sure I've broken this finger. Hurts like hell!'

'I'm *starving*!'

'It was all worth it, though, wasn't it?'

'Sure was, mate. It sure was.'

And there was Beth, struggling back to shore, knocked off her feet by a larger wave and being swept directly towards Luke.

He caught her, helped her to her feet with his arm around her waist, and although they were both standing in only ankle-deep water, he didn't let her go.

He couldn't.

'We've done it, Beth! The whales are safe.'

'I know.' She was smiling. The deep, dark blue eyes

that Luke remembered so well were shining with joy. Even tears, perhaps.

'Willy's back out there with his mum, probably having breakfast. Are you happy?'

'It's fantastic. Of course I'm happy.'

But her smile was fading and those *were* tears in her eyes. And Luke just couldn't bear it. He pulled her closer, wrapping his arms around her and holding her shivering body against his own. Pressing his lips into the wet, salty tresses clinging to the top of her head.

Would Beth have turned her face up towards his like that if she hadn't wanted him to kiss her?

Would he have *wanted* to kiss her if he'd known what it would be like?

If he'd known that the lock would disintegrate on that part of his heart that had been so well protected for so long? That all the old feelings would still be there so completely?

Except they hadn't been complete, had they? Because now he could add the painfully gained wisdom of many years. And forgiveness for the way Beth had ended their relationship and—most importantly—he could add the understanding of why it had happened.

They were both in danger of hypothermia as they stood there in the shallows, but Luke couldn't stop kissing Beth. His hands held her close, his lips moved over hers very gently. This wasn't about passion, although that was potentially only a heartbeat away. It was about finding a connection again and asking whether that connection could ever mean enough to make it worth exploring further.

Luke would have been more than happy to stand there holding Beth for as long as it took. However, the rude shock of having someone else losing their balance in the surf and barrelling into them made it totally impossible to keep his hold on her.

And maybe it was just as well because a familiar voice was shouting from the dry sand. Maureen had some extra clothes. Some nice warm track pants and a woollen jersey.

'I've got a towel here, too, Beth. Come and get dried off, for heaven's sake, before you catch your death.'

The towel felt like sandpaper on skin so cold it felt scorched. Beth's fingers had no chance of undoing the zip on her jeans or even pulling a sodden anorak and sweatshirt off over her head.

Luke had gone off towards the fire on hearing his name being shouted, but Maureen was still there, thank goodness, clucking over Beth like a mother hen and helping her into a soft jersey and some track pants long since discarded by one of her grown children.

'There you go, love. Goodness me, you're cold, aren't you? You sound like you're going to break your teeth, shivering that hard.' The older nurse looked more closely at Beth. 'You're awfully pale. Are you all right?'

Beth simply nodded. And smiled. Because she'd never felt more all right in her life. The exhaustion didn't matter. The bruises and scrapes and strains were insignificant. Even that pain in her side was perfectly tolerable.

Luke had *kissed* her.

Really kissed her. And his lips had told her something she could never have guessed. That he still cared.

Maybe there was a way to get past the hurt they had caused each other. Her fears might have been groundless, given the fact that the man Luke was today bore so little resemblance to the high-flyer she had known. He might have a new perspective on more than just his career these days. He might understand why she had been afraid and be able to see that it hadn't been because she'd thought he hadn't been 'good enough'.

The kiss had told her something else as well. Beth had realised the physical attraction was still there for her. In spades, given the reaction she'd suffered seeing him in the staff pool.

She knew she still loved him, given the fear that it might have been illness that had made him change his lifestyle so drastically. What she hadn't guessed was that the depth of the love she had once felt for Luke had gained an extra dimension even while she had been so busy trying to deny it.

Ever since she had come to Hereford, Beth had been seeing a version of Luke that had all the good qualities she remembered and none of the bad ones. If he'd set out, in fact, to make himself the perfect man for Beth, he couldn't have done a better job.

Maureen was stuffing Beth's wet clothing into a plastic bag.

'Come near the fire and warm up,' she instructed Beth. 'We'll get you something hot to eat and drink and then I'll take you home. Or have you got your car up the hill as well?'

Beth shook her head. She was still shivering hard enough to make speech difficult.

Maureen sounded puzzled. 'So how did you get here?'

Shaking her head had made trickles of sea water run down into Beth's eyes and they stung. Beth screwed her eyes shut and used an almost dry corner of the towel to try and blot the moisture from her dripping scalp.

'I walked.'

'Oh?'

Beth looked up at the tone and Maureen smiled at her.

'Don't worry, I won't tell anybody what I saw.'

The blush had the welcome effect of heating Beth up from the inside and the violent shivering abated. 'There's nothing to tell,' she said. 'Not really. We were all happy, that's all.'

Looking over her shoulder out to sea, Beth could just see the dark shapes of whale fins in the distance beneath a hovering helicopter. Looking ahead of her, she could see people crowding the edges of the bonfire and somewhere in that laughing, talking group would be Luke.

Beth was still happy. She felt oddly dizzy as she started the short trek across the sand and she was more than happy to take a seat on one of the boulders. Someone offered her a piping hot bacon sandwich but Beth shook her head.

'I'm really not hungry, thanks. I'll eat later.'

'Coffee? Or tea? How about some hot chocolate?'

'No, thanks. I'm fine, honestly.'

She wasn't shivering any more. The bonfire was extraordinarily hot, in fact. Beth could feel herself starting to perspire and the odd dizzy feeling increased. Maybe she should have something to eat after all, even if she didn't feel like it.

'I think I will go and find a sandwich,' she told Maureen.

Her legs felt like jelly and Beth regretted her decision to stand up, but Maureen was watching so she made an effort to shake off her physical weakness. She hadn't done any more than anyone else here during the night. It would seem rather pathetic if she collapsed into a heap and fell asleep on the sand now, and Beth did not want to appear pathetic. Not when there was every possibility that Luke could be watching her.

Walking was even more of an effort and Beth's vision blurred slightly. Not enough for her not to recognise Luke, however. Or the blonde woman hanging round his neck like a human pendant as they stood on the edge of the parking area.

Maree appeared to be crying. And Luke looked absolutely terrible. He disentangled himself from the woman's arms and helped her into the passenger seat of his black Jeep. Then he turned back towards the beach.

He saw Beth, she was sure he did, but he stared at her as though he'd never seen her before in his life. For a second he bowed his head, his forehead resting in one hand, as though whatever he was thinking about was unbearable. And then he shook his head, very slowly, and turned to get behind the wheel of the Jeep.

Beth watched the vehicle climb the shingle road up the hill. Away from Boulder Bay beach.

Away from her.

Any joy from the successful rescue mission of the whales and the kiss she had shared with Luke vanished. Its place was filled instantly by sheer misery—both physical and emotional. Fighting back a flood of tears, Beth retraced the few steps she had taken.

'Maureen? I really need to get home and get some sleep before I fall over. Can I take you up on that offer of a lift, please?'

Sleep hadn't helped one little bit.

The exhausted slumber had lasted until well into the

afternoon but Beth woke to find herself feeling extremely unwell.

Her head ached so badly it took a huge effort to get it off the pillow. She was bathed in sweat. Her heart pounded and it felt like there simply wasn't enough air in the room. When she tried to sit and then stand up, Beth became so faint that black spots danced before her eyes and a roaring sound came from nowhere and rushed in to engulf her.

Lying down again, Beth closed her eyes and tried to slow her breathing. This couldn't be the aftermath of exhaustion or even hypothermia. Something was very wrong with her. A bad dose of flu, maybe. She hurt all over. Her joints ached, her whole abdomen was painful and even her skin felt raw.

What time of day was it? Beth rolled onto her side and found her watch on the bedside table. Five o'clock. But it was too light to be 5 a.m. Why was she asleep at 5 p.m.? She was supposed to be at work at 6 p.m., wasn't she?

Panic elbowed space in the confusion and Beth gave up trying to figure it out. She needed some help. Sitting up more carefully this time, she took a few sips of water from the glass beside her watch. Then she picked up her mobile phone, but the screen was blank and the connection for the charger lay on the floor.

Beth tried to insert the little pin into the socket on the back of the phone but it just didn't seem to fit any more and she was horrified to find tears of frustration welling.

This was ridiculous. OK, she wasn't feeling well but she wasn't a small child and she could look after herself. She didn't need her mother, or anyone else, to come running to care for her. So why did she have this overwhelming urge to be cradled in someone's arms right now? To close her eyes and have someone tell her that everything was going to be all right?

Not just someone.

Luke.

Now Beth did begin to cry. She wanted Luke. She needed him. And he wasn't there. He never would be there because he was with someone else. Maree. The good friend.

Snatches of the jumbled dreams she had just been having returned. There was a beach with impossibly bright diamonds of light dancing in the surf. She and Luke were swimming effortlessly in the clear, green water. They were naked. Twisting and turning like dolphins. Touching. With their lips, their hands…their entire bodies.

But she had clothes on now. Weird clothes. Baggy old track pants and a well-worn jersey. Where had they come from? And why had she been in bed with clothes on, anyway? No wonder she had been sweaty and feeling dreadful.

She was feeling better now. She could stand up. Walk even. It was almost like floating. She could see the door of the motel's office. Why was she here?

Oh, yes. She needed to use the phone. To call Luke and tell him she needed him.

No. Beth stopped and shook her head. That wasn't right. She mustn't do that even if she couldn't quite remember why.

She turned but had no idea what she was supposed to do next. Easier to just keep floating. Her feet seemed to know where they wanted to go.

A loud noise hurt her ears. Blaring and unpleasant.

Beth put her hands over her ears but she could still hear the shouting.

'What the *hell* do you think you're doing, woman? You're in the middle of the *road*.'

The voice was familiar. Beth tried hard and found she could open her eyes. She tried to focus on the owner of the furious voice.

'You *idiot*! I could have *killed* you!'

Luke.

The word was in her head. Her lips moved but no sound came from Beth's mouth.

'Beth?' Luke's face was swimming into view now. 'My God, Beth! What on earth's the matter?'

He looked pale. Tired. And very, very sad. Beth reached out her hand to touch him. To let him know that everything was going to be all right.

But her hand reached into nothingness and that floating sensation had gone. She was being sucked down now. Taken away from Luke and swallowed by the waiting blackness.

Very faintly, she could hear a horrified echo of her name.

'Beth!'

CHAPTER EIGHT

NOTHING much could faze Senior Nurse Maureen Skinner.

She'd seen so many and varied emergencies coming through those automatic doors into Ocean View's A and E department she could cope with anything.

Mind you, the car that had come through those very doors recently had been one out of the box, but it hadn't been nearly as alarming as what she was now seeing.

'Luke!' Maureen dropped the file she was holding and ran towards the surgeon. It wasn't until she met him halfway across the tiled reception area that she recognised the face on the limp figure he held in his arms. 'It's *Beth*,' she cried in horror. 'What's happened?'

Luke kept moving towards the resuscitation rooms. 'I found her standing in the middle of the road just outside the car park. She looked totally out of it and then collapsed. Completely unresponsive, and I can't find a radial pulse.'

He laid his burden down on the bed with extraordinary care. It was good clinical practice to tilt Beth's head back and maintain an open airway, but Maureen had never seen a doctor brush loose strands of hair from a patient's face quite like that. Not that this was the time to process such information.

'She's tachypnoeic.' Maureen estimated the rate of Beth's shallow breathing to be well above normal. Close to forty breaths a minute probably. 'I'll get some oxygen on.'

Luke had pushed up the loose sleeve of the old pullover to wrap a blood-pressure cuff around Beth's upper arm. 'Where's Mike?'

'In the small theatre, cleaning out a dog-bite wound.' Maureen slipped an oxygen mask over Beth's face, turned the flow up to ten litres and clipped an oxygen saturation probed over a finger. She could feel the clamminess of Beth's skin and her anxiety level increased sharply as she noticed what looked like a touch of cyanosis darkening the younger nurse's lips. 'I'll get him,' she said tersely.

Luke simply nodded, his gaze fixed on the mercury slipping down inside the sphygmomanometer. 'Unrecordable,' she heard him mutter as she left the area swiftly. 'My God, Beth…what's going on here?'

Maureen returned with Mike seconds later, a house surgeon right behind them, having left Chelsea to complete the dressing and bandaging of the dog-bite wound.

'She's in shock,' Luke informed the emergency department consultant. 'Tachycardic at 130, BP is unrecordable and her oxygen saturation is down to ninety-four per cent.'

'What happened?'

'We don't know.'

'She was out with that whale rescue last night, wasn't she?'

It was Maureen who answered. 'I took her home

about seven o'clock this morning. She said she was just very tired but she didn't *look* well.' She picked up a pair of shears. "She was very pale and she had refused anything to eat or drink before we left.' Maureen was cutting away the pullover. 'She hasn't even changed her clothes. These are the dry ones I gave her at the beach.'

'Was she injured in any way?' Mike had his stethoscope on Beth's chest.

'She didn't appear to be when I spoke to her last.' Luke caught Maureen's glance and looked away hurriedly. Did he know she had seen him kissing Beth? That the way they had been clinging to each other had suggested the embrace had been far more significant than the celebratory gesture Beth had made it out to be? 'She was very cold,' Luke said quickly, 'but we all were by then.'

'Equal air entry and no sign of trauma, but she sounds congested.' Mike slung the stethoscope around his neck and reached for a tourniquet. 'Let's get Kelly through for a chest X-ray. This could be a pulmonary embolism.'

It took several seconds for Mike to successfully locate a vein on Beth's arm and he shook his head. 'She's completely shut down. Start another IV on the other side,' he instructed the house surgeon, Seth, 'and get some fluids running. Maureen, I need some blood tubes. A full biochemistry screen to start with and...' Mike frowned. 'Let's do a coagulation profile and cultures as well. She could well be septic. What's her temperature?'

Maureen put the kidney dish full of blood-test tubes on the bed beside Mike. 'I'll find a thermometer.'

'Is she wearing a medical alert bracelet?'

'No.'

The radiographer arrived to take the chest X-ray and

the other staff members moved briefly behind the lead-lined screen.

'Does anyone know anything of her medical history?' Mike asked. 'Luke?'

Maureen was holding the tympanic thermometer she hadn't had a chance to use yet. 'She's never said anything but, then, she's only been here for a short time, hasn't she?'

'I knew her years ago, Maureen,' Luke said. 'We worked together in south Auckland. But, no, she didn't appear to have any major health issues then.'

Was he avoiding any eye contact with her, Maureen wondered, or was there another reason why Luke's gaze was fixed so firmly on Beth's still figure on the other side of the heavy glass?

Definitely another reason, she decided on hearing him sigh almost inaudibly and watching the way he raked his hair back from his forehead with stiff fingers. She had never seen Luke look this perturbed before.

His colleague's distress hadn't escaped Mike. 'You shouldn't be here, mate,' he said quietly. 'Go home.'

Luke's head shake was terse. 'Not yet. Not until we know what's going on here.'

'It could take a while.'

'I know that.'

Mike cleared his throat. 'I was sorry to hear about your brother-in-law, Luke. Early this morning, wasn't it?'

'Yeah.' Luke's face settled into even grimmer lines. 'Apparently he was watching for the whales from his window. His mum said that as soon as he saw them heading out to sea, he closed his eyes and just stopped breathing.'

Maureen's heart squeezed. No wonder Luke was

looking so perturbed. Even if his connection with Beth was not as significant as she suspected, it would still be too much of a blow to lose another young life right now. She touched Luke's arm with a comforting gesture.

'I saw Maree leaving before the refloating started. Was she there with Kevin at the end?' She could see how hard it was for Luke to swallow.

He nodded grimly. 'I should have been there, too.'

'Maybe you were needed just as much where you were.' Maureen's suggestion was soft and this time Luke's eyes acknowledged what she had seen on the beach, but was the pain she was seeing because of his feelings for Beth? Maybe involving himself to this degree here was simply a distraction from the agony of losing his best friend and feeling that he had let Kevin down by not being there at the end.

Mike must have sensed something of what Maureen was wondering. 'How well did you know Beth, Luke?'

His words gave nothing away. 'Well enough, I guess.'

Mike was moving in response to a signal from the X-ray technician. 'Then do stay,' he urged. 'A familiar face could be just what she needs.'

Luke was still there an hour later when the anaesthetist was called down to intubate Beth and put her onto a ventilator after the oxygen levels in her blood dropped to dangerously low levels.

Luke's counterpart, Ocean View's other general surgeon, Len Armstrong, was there as well. 'She's not in the best shape for surgery yet, Mike.'

'We can't afford to wait,' Mike decided grimly. 'The dopamine infusion has at least brought her blood pressure up a bit and we're getting some urine output, thanks to the diuretics.' He glanced towards the ultrasound machine he had been using a short time ago to examine Beth's now rigid abdomen. 'We've started aggressive antibiotic cover but the longer that perforated appendix is in there, the harder this is going to get.'

'Right.' Len turned away. 'I'll head upstairs and get scrubbed, then.'

'Has someone got in touch with her family yet?'

'I can do that,' Maureen offered.

'No. I will.' Luke looked grey with fatigue now. 'And then I'll come upstairs.'

'Only as a spectator, mate.' Len's smile was clearly intended to cover a concern for Luke's state of mind. 'I'm the one who's on call here, remember.'

'I just need to be there.' Luke pushed himself away from his position and paused for a second beside Beth. Reaching out, he laid the back of his fingers, very gently and very briefly, on Beth's cheek.

Maureen saw the glance that passed between Mike and Len. Puzzled and questioning initially and then accepting. They had even less of an idea of what might be happening here than she did but they knew that some connection existed between Luke and this very unexpected and now critically ill patient. And that connection had just markedly increased the urgency and tension of this case.

Seven p.m. on a Friday night.

The address was still the same but what was the chance of finding Beth's parents at home? Luke punched new numbers into the phone, having just hung up from talking to Directory Service.

Nigel and Celia Dawson were highly likely to be out at a social gathering of some description—if they were

even in the country. They were just as likely to be somewhere else, attending one of the numerous international
conferences that needed a star line-up of speakers.

Then again, the Dawsons had to be well into their six-
ties by now. Maybe they had retired and were embrac-
ing a quieter lifestyle. Sure enough, the phone call was
answered on its third ring by a gruff but familiar voice.

'Yes?'

'Mr Dawson?'

'Who wants to know?'

'This is Luke Savage, Mr Dawson. I'm calling from
Ocean View hospital in Hereford.'

'Savage? That name rings a bell. Do I know you?'

'I'm a surgeon, sir.' Old habits died hard, Luke
thought wryly. Like respect for an eminent specialist. 'I
met you several years ago when I was going out with
your daughter.'

'Ah…' Nigel sounded thoughtful. Or possibly disin-
terested.

'It's Beth I'm calling about.'

'Who?'

'Beth.' Being so tired made it easier to keep his tone
even. 'Your daughter,' he added wryly. 'I thought you
should know that she's—'

'Savage,' the older man interrupted. 'Weren't you
the young chap thinking of a career in cardiothoracic?'

'Yes. I wanted to tell you that—'

'And *where* did you say you were calling from
again?'

'Hereford.'

'Where the hell is Hereford? England?'

'No. Marlborough. South Island, New Zealand.'

'Never heard of a cardiothoracic unit down that way.'

'There isn't one. I'm a general surgéon.'

'Oh?' The monosyllable carried a distinct edge of contempt. 'I seem to remember you as a lad who was going somewhere, Savage. You reminded me of myself, in fact.'

'I've got to exactly where I wanted to go, sir.' So Beth hadn't been the only one to pick the unsettling similarity. Luke tried to push away the weariness threatening to allow any further distraction. He didn't care what Nigel Dawson thought of him any more and he certainly wasn't about to start defending his career choices. 'Right now I'm heading up to Theatre where your daughter is about to undergo surgery.'

'What the hell is she doing in...Hereford, did you say?'

'She's been working in the emergency department here for a couple of weeks now.'

'First I've heard of it. What's she having surgery for?'

'A perforated appendix. Beth is critically ill right now, Mr Dawson. She's in septic shock and is on life support.'

'Well, she shouldn't be in a tin-pot hospital in the middle of nowhere, then, should she? Get a damned helicopter and ship her out, son. What's the closest tertiary centre? Dunedin? Wellington?'

'Beth couldn't possibly be moved right now. She's far too ill.'

'It should have been done earlier, then, shouldn't it? Who's in charge down there?'

Luke ignored the bluster. 'We're doing everything that can be done,' he said firmly. 'And we have excellent intensive care facilities available.'

He could hear another voice in the background. A female voice, calling for Nigel. Maybe Beth's mother would be more appropriately concerned with her child's state of health rather than her whereabouts or finding someone to blame for her condition.

'You should be able to get a commercial flight to Nelson,' Luke said into the silent line. 'It'll take about ninety minutes by road from there. Otherwise there are small airlines operating out of Hereford airport.'

'I can't go to Hereford.' Nigel sounded astonished at the suggestion. 'I'm about to take a flight to Rome. I'm the keynote speaker at a conference that's due to kick off in less than twenty-four hours. The taxi's here now, as a matter of fact.' The voice became fainter, as though the phone was being held at arm's length. 'I'll be there in a second, darling.'

'Perhaps I could speak to Beth's mother?'

'There's no time for that. We're going to miss our flight at this rate.'

A wash of something like desperation hit Luke and he closed his eyes for a moment. Her parents were strangers, Beth had said. She had never known the kind of love Luke had been blessed with from family and friends. Could Luke ever hope to make up for that? Would she trust him enough to let him try?

'Look. I'll pass the message on.' Nigel's tone was dismissive. 'I suppose I'd better try and let that young man know what's going on as well. Or is he down there already?'

Luke's eyes opened smartly. 'Who?'

'Her fiancé, of course. Brent what's-his-name. Ranger or Granger, maybe.'

The heaviness engulfing Luke became unbearable. It was an effort to draw in a deep breath. 'I was under the impression that Beth's engagement had ended before she came to Hereford.'

'News to me. Mind you, I haven't actually spoken to the girl since she stormed out of here that day. When was it, two years ago? I hear any news secondhand, through her brother or that Brent chap. She's the worst of the lot as far as keeping in touch.'

'I wonder why?' Luke muttered.

'Pardon?'

Luke cleared his throat, suddenly more than ready to end this conversation. 'Please, do pass the message on to anyone who may be concerned about Beth's welfare.' He wasn't worried that his criticism might not be veiled well enough to avoid causing Nigel offence. He might find out whether the man actually cared a fig for his daughter. 'Rest assured that we will be taking the best possible care of her in the meantime.'

'Good lad.' Beth's father sounded relieved at the opportunity to abdicate any responsibility. 'You do that.'

Not that there was much that Luke could do except to be there for Beth. The effort that took, however, made it possibly the hardest thing he'd ever done in his life.

Never before had he felt like this in any operating room. Every unusual blip on the cardiac monitor—and there were plenty as the anaesthetist struggled to keep Beth's blood pressure at a level that could sustain life—made his own heart skip a beat and then start racing in alarm. He had to look away from the initial incision because it made him feel physically sick. This was Beth's flesh being cut.

Luke's professional side noted how well Len was dealing with the surgery. The caecum was identified. The appendicular artery was secured, clamped, divided and ligated. The appendix mesentery was divided. The nasty, swollen and infected appendix was clamped with artery forceps and removed with care to avoid it spilling any more of its poison into the surrounding tissues and blood vessels.

But that damage had already occurred and it was no less nerve-racking for Luke to be beside Beth's bed after she was transferred to the intensive care unit. Her blood pressure was still marginal and the function of vital organs like her kidneys and lungs was severely compromised. Central venous pressures were being monitored by a Swan-Ganz catheter, which had been threaded right through her heart to rest in a section of her pulmonary artery and Beth was kept intubated and ventilated.

The consultant now in charge of her care was more than a little concerned about her renal function, but Luke was only half listening to the professional interchanges as he sat there holding Beth's hand and talking quietly to her whenever her medical attendants were occupied with the machinery rather than with Beth's body.

'I'm here, Beth,' he whispered, time after time. 'You're going to be all right.'

Barbara came up to the unit just after midnight, and Luke left Beth's side to meet his mother on the other side of the double swing doors.

'What are doing here, Mum? Is everything all right?'

'I was worried about you, love,' Barbara told her son. 'Nobody would tell my anything except that you were keeping a sick friend company.'

'I'm sorry,' Luke said sincerely. 'I should have called. I should be with you at the Winsomes' but I lost track of time.'

'It's all right.'

'I can't leave Beth just yet. It's still touch and go.'

'Of course you can't, darling.' Barbara squeezed his hand.

How could she know? Luke wondered. How he *really* felt about Beth when he hadn't known himself until faced with the prospect of losing her like this? He'd lost track of time all right, because minute by minute his feelings for this woman were growing stronger. He *wasn't* going to lose her.

He *couldn't*.

'How is she?'

'Not good. She waited too long to get help. The infection has really taken hold. We'll just have to hope the antibiotics kick in soon.'

'But she *is* going to make it, isn't she?'

'I hope so, Mum.' For just a split second Luke lost control and fear tangled its icy fingers around his heart just a shade more tightly. Had he found Beth again and been given the possibility of making things right just in time to lose her for ever?

Was it somehow *his* fault that he lost the people he loved the most?

'This is *not* your fault, Luke,' Barbara said softly. 'None of it. Not Jodie or Kevin. Or Beth. And Beth's going to be fine, I'm sure of it.'

Luke couldn't go there. Not right now. 'How's Maree?' he asked. 'And Joan?'

'Coping. John brought his flight from Sydney forward and he arrived early this evening. Kevin's come back from the funeral parlour. We're going to keep him at home until the funeral on Monday. The vicar's been to visit. All the arrangements are made now.' Barbara's smile wobbled. 'Kevin and Jodie are finally going to be together again.'

'Did you remember the tape I made? The music Kev wanted?'

'It's all done. Joan said to say thank you.'

'I'll get in to see everybody just as soon as I can.'

'They understand why you're here, Luke. It's OK.'

'Do they?' Luke ran a hand over his eyes. 'I'm not sure I understand myself. I haven't seen Beth for six years. How can I feel like this when she's only been back in my life for a matter of days?'

'I think you always felt like this.' Barbara smiled. 'You just did a very good job of hiding it. From everyone, yourself included.'

'So how come you guessed?'

'I'm your mother. It's my job to know about stuff like that.' Barbara had to reach up a long way to stroke her son's hair. 'You need some sleep. And you need to stay with Beth. She needs you more than Kevin does right now. And who knows? Maybe he's here somewhere, practising a bit of guardian angel stuff.'

Luke hoped so. He managed to return his mother's smile but the moment she turned and stepped into the lift his face crumpled and he had to scrub the burning pain of tears from his eyes with both palms.

But maybe his mother was right. His thoughts turned often enough to his friend in the quiet moments of the rest of that night, and the feeling of Kevin's presence was strong enough to make him smile at times. He wished he could have told his mate that he understood now why Kevin had had no fear of dying. Why life without his soul mate had been so grey.

Luke thought he'd found peace in his own life in the last few years. Happiness, even. But it was so clear now what was still missing, and the only person who would be able to fill that gap was lying on the hospital bed beside him with tubes and wires snaking from her body, attaching her to machines that were, hopefully, improving her chances for survival.

And those chances needed to improve, dammit. Right now they were probably about fifty-fifty and the odds were terrifying. Luke covered one of the small, cool hands on the bed with both of his own.

'I'm here, Beth,' he whispered yet again. 'You're going to be all right.'

It seemed so wrong that it was Luke receiving the visitors at the intensive care unit and not Beth.

Barbara returned early on Saturday morning with a change of clothes and some shaving gear for Luke, and later on Maree came.

'How's Beth doing? Has there been any change?'

'Not for the better. They're trying some different drugs to see if they can improve her kidney function and she's…well, we're waiting for the results on another set of bloods to see if she needs a transfusion.'

'Why would she need that?'

'There's a thing you can get from septic shock called DIC—disseminated intravascular coagulation. Basically means that the mechanisms that control clotting pack up so the patient can bleed to death.'

'But you don't know that she's got that?'

'No.' Luke ran his hands through his hair. 'But some of the puncture sites seem to be bleeding more than they should be.'

Maree sat on one of the chairs in the relatives' room and patted the one beside her. Luke obediently sat down.

'Does Beth know how much you care about her, Luke?'

He thought of the kiss they'd shared in the surf and started to nod cautiously, but then he remembered the conversation when they had been looking after Willy.

He could hear the angry echo of the list of criticisms he had harboured for so long and the nod turned into a miserable sideways movement. Maybe Beth had responded to that kiss simply because it had represented closure of some sort.

'I don't know, Maree,' he sighed. 'Probably not.'

'Then you'll have to tell her,' Maree said calmly. 'It's possible she can hear you, isn't it? Even if she's unconscious?'

'It's possible,' Luke agreed. It was possible that Beth was aware of the touch of his hand on hers as well. Maybe not in any real sense, more like the way he could feel Kevin's presence. His mate might only be there in his memory but the presence was real enough to matter. Enough to make a difference.

Luke squeezed his eyes tightly shut but couldn't prevent an errant tear from escaping. 'I'm going to miss your big brother,' he told Maree. 'So much.'

Maree just nodded, silent for a minute as she struggled with her own tears. Then her lips twisted into a crooked smile.

'Kev approved, you know.'

'Of what?'

'You and Beth. I told him that you were looking pretty cosy as you looked after that baby whale together. He gave me a thumbs-up sign and I couldn't stop him talking for ages after that.'

'What did he say?'

'Oh, that she was the one for you. I'm supposed to

tell you to do the job properly this time or you'll be the first person he's going to haunt.'

Luke groaned. 'What are we going to do without him?'

'I know what you're going to do.' Maree hugged Luke fiercely as she took her leave. 'You're going to go in there and tell Beth how you feel. Tell her just how much she's got to live for.'

It took an hour to get a private enough moment. Luke had to wait until Beth's consultant had been and gone yet again, having reviewed all available results, adjusted some of the settings on the life-support machinery and ordered another raft of tests. Then the blood-sample technician came and went and finally Beth's nurse, Claire, frowned at the chart.

'Why haven't they been in for that chest X-ray yet? I'd better go and ring. Can you watch Beth for a minute, Luke?'

'Sure.'

He could do more than watch. He took her hand, carefully avoiding the IV port and line taped to the top but managing to twine her fingers with his own. He leaned very close so that his lips brushed her ear.

'I love you, Beth Dawson,' he whispered. 'I didn't realise till now but I never *stopped* loving you.'

He had to pause long enough to swallow the lump in his throat and take a deep breath.

'I always will love you,' he continued softly. 'I hope you can hear me but it doesn't really matter if you can't because you're going to get better and I'm not letting you leave here until you understand just how much I do love you.'

Was it his imagination or did Luke feel a tiny flutter from the fingers laced with his own?

It was probably just that he had to let go of Beth's hand hurriedly as her nurse returned. He was providing enough food for gossip by being here as an old friend for Beth. How much worse would it be if everyone knew how much he was really suffering?

And it was hardly a professional look for those who didn't know him. Like the man wearing a gown and mask to accompany the nurse to Beth's bedside.

'Beth's got a visitor, Luke.' She turned to the newcomer. 'Brent, this is Luke Savage. He's one of our surgeons and a friend of Beth's.'

Luke stood up slowly. Claire hadn't finished her introductions yet. She hesitated just a fraction, as though wondering how Luke was going to react. She was, no doubt, as curious about his relationship with Beth as everybody else probably was.

'This is Brent Granger, Luke,' she said finally. She bit her lip but her tone was calm. Admirably professional. 'Beth's fiancé.'

CHAPTER NINE

STAYING positive was going to be a big ask.

Not on Beth's account, thank goodness. The improved results on all the most recent tests filtered back as Ocean View's ICU consultant arrived to speak to Beth's visitor in the privacy of his office. There was no real reason for Luke to be present other than his delivery of the chest X-ray, which he clipped onto the viewing box and then perused intently.

The consultant shook hands with Brent. 'You're a cardiologist, I hear?'

'That's correct. I'm in private practice at The Sisters of Mercy in Auckland.'

'And you're Beth Dawson's fiancé?'

'Also correct.'

The short silence echoed with the unspoken question of why Beth had come to Hereford if that was the case, but the consultant let go of any curiosity quickly.

'Beth's been a very sick young lady,' he told Brent, 'and I wouldn't say we're entirely out of the woods yet, but we can at least be confident that she's going to pull through this.' He smiled as he scanned the biochemistry report he was holding. 'As you've seen, renal function is almost back to normal and we're definitely onto the right antibiotics.'

'Which are?' Dr Brent Granger's tone was clipped. He could have been speaking to a junior houseman rather than an experienced specialist.

'We're using clindamycin with gentamycin and clox-acillin. We wanted to make sure we were covering any anaerobic organisms as well, of course.'

He glanced up at the X-ray illuminated on the wall. 'Looking good, isn't it, Luke?'

'Hell of a lot better than last night's. Lung fields are almost completely clear.'

'The fluid balance was tricky,' the consultant confessed. 'We had a bit of a juggling act to improve perfusion without aggravating her pulmonary oedema.'

'You've been combining an albumin infusion with diuretic therapy, I suppose?' Brent's gaze left the X-ray and settled on Luke for a split second. Then he, too, was seemingly dismissed as irrelevant.

'Yes. I'm happy enough with her pressures to take out the Swan-Ganz catheter now and we should be able to get her off the ventilator later today. Then it should just be a matter of keeping a close eye on her for a few days.'

'There's no reason she couldn't be transferred within the next day or two, then, is there?' Brent reached to pick up Beth's notes from the desk and began to flick through them.

'I'd prefer to keep her in Intensive Care for another twenty-four hours or so.' The consultant smiled at Brent. 'Then we'll certainly transfer her into our medical ward.'

'No.' Brent shook his head. 'I'm talking about taking her *home*. To Auckland.' The cardiologist certainly had a charming smile but its effect was lost on Luke.

'Beth may prefer to stay in Hereford,' he suggested mildly. 'She might not have been here very long but she's made a lot of friends.'

The flick of a dark eyebrow was subtle but the message was clear. *Like you?* Luke held the eye contact steadily, refusing to be intimidated. *Yes*, he said silently. *Like me.*

'I think discussion about discharge could wait a while yet,' the consultant said.

'Of course.' Brent seemed happy to co-operate. 'The plane I chartered will be here until I have to head back on Monday. That should give us plenty of time.'

'And you have somewhere to stay in Hereford? The hospital has a good relationship with one of the closest motels if—'

Brent waved his hand. 'No need. My secretary made arrangements for me to stay at the Millhouse. I'm hoping that will be quite satisfactory.'

'It should be, at the kind of prices they charge.' Beth's consultant looked amused. 'In any case, perhaps Luke could show you the facilities we have at Ocean View. Beth's going to be asleep for a while yet. You'll need to know where to find our cafeteria and so on. Luke? Have you got the time?'

'Sure.'

The need to get away from the hospital and spend time with his own family and friends would be satisfied very soon. Luke could hardly continue his vigil at Beth's bedside playing musical chairs with her fiancé, could he? He might even try and fit in a walk on a beach because some breathing space was definitely called for here.

It was impossible not to feel alarmed at the turn of events. Luke was quite sure that Beth had been sincere when she had told him her engagement was over, but Brent Granger was clearly a man who was used to getting what he wanted and why would he be here now if he had no interest in reclaiming Beth's affections?

As if he guessed the direction of Luke's thoughts, Brent caught his gaze as soon as they had left the consultant's office.

'I expect you're a bit curious.'

Luke tilted his head fractionally. 'Beth did mention a fiancé. An *ex*-fiancé.'

Brent's confident gaze didn't flicker at all. 'Beth needed a little time to think about things. I'm sure she'll be delighted that I've made the effort to rush to her sickbed.'

It was certainly a lot more than her family had done. The thought that Beth might well be delighted at such an obvious expression of concern was not a pleasant one. If Brent had been looking for a way back into Beth's life, he'd just been handed a golden opportunity here.

Maybe Luke's challenge, given the short time since Beth's arrival in Hereford, was not going to be to convince Beth that he had changed. Or that his love for her was strong enough to give them a future together.

He hadn't expected to be faced with competition from someone who had already come a step closer to marrying Beth than Luke had. Her relationship with Brent was so much more recent as well. Could six-year-old memories measure up in comparison? Could *he* measure up? Luke flicked another glance towards the man walking alongside him as he led Brent towards the lift at the end of the corridor.

Physically, Brent wasn't dissimilar to himself, being just as tall and just as dark. He was older than Luke by a good ten years but if anything that probably gave him an advantage in terms of confidence and sophistication. Not being on duty, Luke was currently wearing the comfortable old jeans and shirt that Barbara had brought in for him. Brent was wearing a pinstripe suit and carrying a briefcase, which made him look far more the part of a consultant than Luke did.

More worrying, however, was the sense of power the man exuded, which could only come from being very successful and probably very wealthy. Combined with that charming smile and an attractive British accent that hinted at a northern upbringing rather than public school, Brent could have stepped from the pages of some romantic novel. It wasn't hard to believe that Beth had accepted a proposal from the cardiologist. What Luke would dearly like to know at that moment was why she'd felt such an urge to escape.

He pushed the button to summon the lift. 'So, how did you meet Beth?'

'I worked in the same London hospital as her older brother, David. When I decided on a sabbatical on this side of the world, I wanted to meet his family.'

'So you're on sabbatical?' A temporary stay, then. This was good.

'It was supposed to only be for a year but Beth wasn't all that happy about the idea of living in London.' Brent's smile at Luke would have been engaging if it wasn't for the underlying hint of triumph. 'I've got a little surprise for her now, though. I've purchased a property and signed a contract for permanent employment at Mercy.'

The lift doors slid shut, trapping the two men in a rather too confined space for Luke's liking. He could smell the aftershave Brent was wearing. It was as inoffensive and subtle as many aspects of this man's personality, so why did they all add up to a force that felt like a human bulldozer?

Because there was steel beneath the silk, that's why. That glance Luke had received when the 'little surprise' had been revealed had carried a disturbing undertone. Brent Granger expected things to go his way. And they would, because he was very charming and generous about setting the process into place. And because he wasn't going to tolerate anything else.

Had Beth simply been railroaded into an engagement? Flattened by charm and confidence and sheer power? If so, what chance would she have of harbouring whatever doubts had caused her to break off the engagement in the first place? Right now, she would be weak enough to be incredibly vulnerable.

Luke didn't like the knot forming in his gut. Beth needed protection but what right did he have to offer it? Brent had stepped into the space he had willingly taken from the moment Beth had collapsed. Maybe neither of them had a right to assume that role, but Luke couldn't compete on the same playing field as Brent. He wouldn't even want to try exerting that kind of control.

Brent cleared his throat into the silence. 'Is there a florist of some kind based in the hospital?'

'The gift shop has some flowers available. We'll go past it on the way to the cafeteria.'

'Good. Beth's parents have asked me to organise something on their behalf.'

Luke kept his tone carefully bland. 'It's a shame they couldn't be here themselves.'

'Mmm.' Brent shook his head sadly. 'Beth's been estranged from her family for some time. In fact, that was how I met her. I was visiting a patient in the hospital she worked in and Nigel and Celia asked me to deliver a birthday gift that was too fragile to post.' He stepped out of the lift ahead of Luke.

'Beth refused to accept it. She actually got rather upset and I ended up taking her out to dinner.'

Luke could feel the tension building in his jaw. This man had started using Beth's vulnerability to his advantage right from the beginning, hadn't he? What woman wouldn't respond to someone taking charge at a time like that?

'She was such a lonely little thing,' Brent added fondly. 'Despite all her friends. What Beth really needs in her life is a family and I'm hoping things between her and her parents will improve. I expect once they've got grandchildren nearby, they'll appreciate what they've been missing.'

Grandchildren?

Brent's children?

An image of Beth holding a baby in her arms sprang into Luke's mind. And then one of her watching over toddlers playing. Brent was right, of course. Beth deserved the security and love a family of her own could provide.

It was what Luke needed in his own life.

He wanted to be a part of that picture he could see so vividly. He wanted to share the joy that a child of their own could bring.

They were passing the gift shop now and Brent paused to look at the display of merchandise.

'The bunches of flowers are a bit on the small side, aren't they? I'll have to buy the lot, I think.'

'Flowers aren't allowed in ICU.'

'They'll be ready for her transfer into the ward, then, won't they?' Brent's smile was satisfied. 'I'll get one of those teddy bears, too. Beth will love that.'

Obviously there was not going to be any shortage of gifts showered on Beth in the foreseeable future. And how long would that be? Brent had a very clear vision of permanence, it seemed, and Beth was a key player. Would his generosity make her any more receptive to his plans?

And was there anything Luke could do about it if it did?

He couldn't stay in the hospital all day. He was needed elsewhere. But leaving Beth to wake up and find Brent beside her was more than unsettling.

The cardiologist seemed to sense how torn Luke felt. He held out his hand and Luke was forced to shake it.

'Thanks for your help, old chap,' Brent said politely, 'but don't let me hold you up any longer. I'll be just fine now.'

Luke's feet felt like lead as he headed towards the car park.

It would be Brent sitting beside Beth when she finally opened her eyes later today. Even if she had been aware of a loving presence beside her for the last twenty-four hours, she couldn't possibly be certain of his identity. He himself may have been giving her messages of love that Brent would now be credited with, and there was nothing Luke could do about it without potentially making a fool of himself.

He had never felt so powerless in his life but he was just too damned tired to try and think of a way of redressing the situation.

The needs of others were calling him away from a

selfish focus in any case. Kevin's family…his own family…needed comfort.

Still being tired wasn't enough to stop Luke rising early to go into the hospital on Sunday morning. The Millhouse was well away from Ocean View and surely Brent wouldn't have time to have breakfast and go visiting by 7 a.m. Finding Beth alone with her nurse was a good start.

'How is she, Claire?'

'Doing great. She's been off the ventilator since 4 p.m. yesterday and everything's looking good. They'll be shifting her into the ward today, I would think.'

'Has she been awake much?'

'She stirred a little at odd times overnight, but hasn't said anything yet.'

The knot in Luke's gut unravelled just a little. She hadn't spoken to Brent yet, then. He still had a chance to say something. To at least tell her that he loved her.

Claire smiled and Luke was sure she had guessed his thoughts. 'I'll leave you two alone for a minute,' she said. 'I'll just be in the office if you need me.'

Luke sat down on the chair and took Beth's hand. The IV line was still there but he could see the fluids were drug-free. It was just normal saline, keeping the line open and her fluid levels up. Her skin felt warm but not febrile, and while Beth's face was still very pale she looked a whole lot better.

Luke squeezed her hand. 'I told you everything would be all right, didn't I?' he asked softly. 'I'm still here, Beth.' He swallowed hard. 'And I still love you, sweetheart.'

His thumb traced slow circles on Beth's palm and it

was no imagined flicker he felt in her fingers this time. They curled around his softly. A weak grip but definitely a grip. Luke watched her face intently as her eyelashes fluttered and the corners of her lips twitched into a tiny smile. She was surfacing from a deep sleep. Any moment now she would open her eyes and when they managed to focus, it would be Luke she saw sitting so close.

The return of Claire was unexpected and she sounded as apologetic as she looked.

'I'm so sorry, Luke, but ED is wondering if you could go down?'

'I'm not on call, Claire.'

'They know that. There's someone there who's asking for you.'

'Who?' Beth's eyelashes were still again, black against her pale cheeks. Her fingers lay still also. Had the buzz of conversation been enough to send her back into exhausted slumber?

'Joan Winsome? Is she a relative?'

'What's Joan doing in Emergency?'

'Her daughter's been brought in by ambulance. Apparently she collapsed at home this morning.'

'Oh…*God*!' There was no help for it. Luke felt like he was tearing off part of his own flesh as he extracted his hand from Beth's and stood up. He walked towards the exit of the intensive care unit without looking back. He couldn't afford to look back or it would be far too hard to keep moving.

The dream was fading.

Beth tried to hang onto it but instead of being cradled in Luke's arms she was running now. Her bare feet sank into the warmth of dry sand and the soothing rhythm of breaking surf became fainter. Where was Luke? All she could see were the smooth, dark shapes of boulders. She tried to call because she could hear her name, but her lips refused to co-operate and her feet were slowing. She was just too tired to keep running.

'Beth! Wake up, darling.'

Luke! Beth made a huge effort to surface from the dream. Luke was calling her. He was calling her *darling*. Her eyelids felt too heavy to open and there was pain. Her head thumped and there was a sharper pain in her belly. But the effort was worthwhile because Luke was there. She could see the outline of his dark head. She just needed to blink so that her vision would be clear enough to see those beloved dark eyes.

Except…they were the wrong colour. Green instead of grey. Weird. And the voice wasn't quite right either. Beth blinked again.

'Brent…what are *you* doing here?'

'I came to look after you, darling.'

'But…where…?' Where's Luke? Beth wanted to cry, but her head swam with sudden confusion and she had to close her eyes again to try and sort it out. 'Where am I?'

'You're in the intensive care unit, Beth. You had a perforated appendix and a nasty dose of septicaemia. But don't worry, you're on the mend now. Everything's going to be all right.'

Of course everything was going to be all right. Luke had been saying that all along.

Or had he? Had Beth simply been dreaming all along? Creating some sort of fantasy fuelled by fever and drugs?

'You're well enough to go to the ward now,' Brent told her. 'And I've arranged to take you back to

Auckland tomorrow so I can take care of you while you recuperate.'

'No…' Beth pulled her eyes open again. 'You can't…do that.'

'I already have.' Brent patted her hand. 'There'll be a few people annoyed at not getting their slot for elective angioplasty and another couple that'll have to wait for their permanent pacemakers, but I didn't want to rush you, darling. We've scheduled take off for 2 p.m. tomorrow.'

Beth tried to shake her head but it was easier to lie still. She didn't want to go home. She *was* home. Surely she could stay where she was until she felt better?

'It's kind of you, Brent, but I don't want to go back to Auckland. And I don't need looking after. I can take care of myself.'

'Not just yet you can't. I want to look after you, Beth. You know that.'

'Brent…' Beth summoned the last of her strength. 'I've already told you I can't marry you. I don't love you. I don't understand why you're here.'

'I'm not doing this to blackmail you in some way, Beth. I just want you to get better. We'll talk about other things later.'

'No.' But Beth knew she had no hope of winning this so she gave up for the moment and left her eyes shut. She wanted Brent to go away, but if he wasn't going to then she would just escape and go back to that dream. She welcomed the reprieve of unconsciousness enfolding her. This time she would find Luke.

'I don't believe it. It *can't* be true.'

'Why not?' Luke was smiling. 'It makes sense, doesn't it? You've been feeling off colour ever since you got here and Mum's been very worried about you not eating.'

'But why now? We're not on the list for more IVF for another three months. It's *been* three months since the last attempt. I've been trying to get pregnant for *years*, Luke. Why would happen all by itself and why now?'

'Maybe it's the best time it could have happened, Maree. It's going to give us all something special to celebrate.'

'I can't tell anybody. Not till after the funeral. It wouldn't be fair.'

'On whom?' Luke's smile was poignant now. 'Kevin? He'd be as happy as you should be about this, love. On your mum? She's just lost her son. Don't you think the biggest comfort she could have would be that her first grandchild is on the way?'

'A grandson.' Maree's husband, John, was holding his wife's hand tightly and still had a rather bemused smile on his face. 'I can't believe we could see him so clearly on that scan.'

'Joan's still in the waiting room,' Luke reminded them. 'Can I tell her she can come in now?'

'You tell her, John.'

'Shall I tell her the news?'

Maree nodded. 'Luke's right. And Kev was the world's worst at keeping secrets, wasn't he?'

'And then we'll get you home,' Luke said firmly. 'You need rest and some fluids to deal with your dehydration. It's no wonder you fainted, with your blood pressure dropping like that when you stand up.'

Maree was reaching for the leather handbag John had left on her bed when he'd gone to find his mother-in-law. She fished inside.

'Can you get rid of these for me, please, Luke?'

Luke accepted the packet of cigarettes. 'Have you got those patches with you?'

'Don't need them,' Maree said decisively. 'This is the best incentive I could ever get for stopping smoking, and I'm not going to use anything that might be harmful to the baby.'

Luke smiled as he squashed the half-full packet and dropped it into the rubbish bin. 'Good for you, love. You'll do it, too, I know you will.'

He excused himself before Joan came to see Maree in her cubicle. The small family needed time by themselves to absorb the startling discovery that a new member was expected. And he needed time to go back and see if Beth was awake yet.

Luke.

Beth blinked at the man beside her bed. How could she have been wrong…again? She had been so sure Luke was there. That wonderful feeling of comfort had come back. Of safety.

Of knowing she was exactly where she wanted to be.

But it was still Brent sitting beside her bed.

'You're awake again, darling. How are you feeling?'

'Better. Thirsty.'

'There's iced water. Here, let me help you sit up a bit.' Brent slid his arm behind Beth. 'And look—you've got a visitor.'

Beth looked. Luke was standing at the foot of her bed, her chart in his hand, and suddenly it felt terribly wrong to have Brent's arm supporting her as she sat up enough to be able to swallow safely.

'Luke…'

'Hi.' His smile was so much better in real life than it had been in her dreams. So was the look in those dark, grey eyes. It was just the kind of look Beth most wanted to see. The one that made her feel as though she was the most important thing in the world. The most loved even.

'You're looking a lot better,' Luke said. 'That's great.'

Beth couldn't look away from him. But why was he reading her chart? Had he come to visit as a doctor rather than anything personal? 'Was it you that took my appendix out, Luke?'

'No.' Luke smiled. 'They wouldn't have let me do that.'

'Why not?'

'I...wasn't on call. And we were all a bit tired after that rescue effort.'

'What rescue effort?' Brent was looking from Beth to Luke and back again, and he didn't look happy.

'The whales,' Beth told him. Her gaze flew back to Luke. 'Were they all right? They didn't try and strand themselves again, did they?'

'They hung around for a while but they haven't been seen since Friday afternoon.'

'Here, darling. Drink this.'

Beth obediently took a sip from the glass of water Brent was holding to her lips, but she shook her head when he tried again. She didn't want another drink. She didn't want Brent to be here at all, in fact. She didn't want anybody to be here except Luke, but that was just wishful thinking. The numbers around her bed increased further as Claire and another nurse arrived.

'We're all set for you in the ward,' she told Beth. 'We were just waiting for you to wake up. I'm sorry, but we don't have any private rooms available. You'll be sharing with Mrs Daniels, who's just had her gall bladder out.'

'Oh.' The sound was pure disappointment. No chance of any private time with Luke in the ward either, then. Beth still felt weak enough for the frustration to bring tears to her eyes.

'It's only for tonight,' Brent said soothingly. 'It's just as well I'm going to whisk you back tomorrow to that luxury suite at the Mercy to finish recuperating.'

Beth blinked back the tears. To her dismay her voice was slower to get into line and her words came out sounding far less sure than she had intended. 'I said I didn't want to go to Auckland, Brent.'

'I don't think she should go either,' Luke said.

Beth caught her breath. Maybe they didn't need any private time. If Luke felt anything like she did then he could just say something right now. If she had been sure about how *he* felt, *she* would have said something already.

But Luke's words were disappointingly professional. 'Beth's not nearly well enough to travel yet.'

'That's why I've organised a medivac flight,' Brent said coolly. 'And hired a medical escort.' He smiled at Beth. 'I've even organised some tickets so that your friend can pop over from Melbourne for a visit. You'd like to see Neroli, wouldn't you?'

'Of course, but—'

'No "buts",' Brent said firmly. 'It's all organised. Your job is to just rest and get better.'

Say something, Luke, Beth pleaded silently. Claire was releasing the brakes on her bed. Things were happening too fast and she didn't have the strength to resist by herself.

'You should see all the flowers in your room,' Claire said. 'Mrs Daniels says it's like being in the middle of a florist's shop. All the nurses are dead jealous.'

Had Luke sent flowers? Beth tried to thank him with her eyes but to her dismay he dropped his gaze and stood back to make room for the bed.

Brent was smiling broadly. 'It's no more than you deserve, darling. And it's only the beginning.'

Beth lost sight of Luke as her bed was wheeled away. It felt far more like an end than any beginning.

CHAPTER TEN

THE MUSIC MADE people smile through their tears.

'Trust Kev,' someone murmured. 'Who else would try and make us laugh at his own funeral?'

'It was a beautiful service. Are you staying for the lunch?'

'Of course.' The speaker waved at the person walking towards them. 'Yoo-hoo, Luke! You're coming back to the house, aren't you?'

Luke paused near the elderly relatives. 'I'll be there within an hour or so. I've got someone I really need to pop in and see at the hospital on my way.'

'Ah!' Kevin s aunt nodded gravely. 'I hope your patients know how lucky they are to have you, Luke.'

The corner of Luke's mouth curled into a brief, lopsided smile. 'That's what I intend to find out, actually.'

Aunty Pru looked puzzled but Luke moved on. Joan waved to him from a distance, knowing his mission, and Maree used the hand that wasn't holding tightly to John's to give him an encouraging thumbs-up signal.

The Jeep rumbled into life but Luke gripped the steering-wheel and stayed motionless for several seconds while he took a very deep breath.

The service *had* been beautiful. A celebration of life…and love. Luke's twin sister, Jodie, had been spoken of almost as much as Kevin, and the presence of the young lovers had felt real enough to add a sharp poignancy to the powerful mix of emotions.

It had been real enough for Luke to actually hear things Kevin had said so recently.

That not many people were lucky enough to find their soul mate.

That Beth had been the only one who had ever made Luke consider marriage.

That Beth still cared.

That Luke could find a way to flip that coin if he wanted to.

That Beth was *the* one for him.

And that he'd better do the job properly this time.

By the time the final hymn had been sung, Luke had known with absolute conviction that he couldn't let Brent win. It would be wrong for Beth. Brent Granger was the epitome of what Luke had once aspired to be himself. Successful. Powerful. In control of his own life and the lives of those who shared it.

And he was planning to whisk Beth back to his own territory, no matter what she might prefer. How much more in control would he be then?

Beth deserved better than that.

Having just been reminded so vividly how precious relationships were, Luke was not going to lose the woman he loved so much. Not if there was any chance at all that she might feel the same way, and there had to be a chance.

She wouldn't have reacted as she had about raking

up the past that time he'd suggested coffee if he didn't still have an effect on her.

He'd definitely felt something touch his soul that time their eyes had met after he'd commented on those awful rabbit slippers.

And why had she been coming to his house when she'd discovered the stranded whales if she hadn't had the intention of spending time alone with him?

She had *kissed* him, for God's sake. And that connection had taken Luke back in time. Right back to when he had first realised he had fallen in love with Beth. Before he'd met her parents. Before he'd rushed blindly into imposing his own vision of a future that had so missed the real point of being together.

He knew where he had gone so wrong. He knew that he was on the right track now. Somehow he had to let Beth know that.

The big stainless-steel meal trolley was filling the lift so Luke took the stairs to the medical ward on the second floor of Ocean View hospital two at a time.

Please… The word became a mantra. Please, let Beth be alone. If he was lucky enough, Brent would be finding some lunch of his own in the cafeteria by now. What time *had* they planned to leave?

When he entered the room with Beth's name on the door and saw the empty bed, Luke felt the shock like a physical blow.

He was too late.

Beth had been spirited away back to Auckland and it would be much harder to find and talk to her now. Maybe she would just refuse to speak to him when he tried.

And he would deserve the reaction because he should have been more sure of himself. And of Beth. Kevin had been right. She *was* the one. Luke could feel the connection so strongly that Beth would surely believe him even if she wasn't so sure herself, and any belief would give them the chance to try again and this time Luke knew they couldn't possibly go wrong because he simply wouldn't allow them to.

'Hi, Luke.' The soft voice came from the depths of the armchair positioned over by the windows.

'Beth!' Luke's breath rushed out in a huge sigh of relief as his head jerked sideways. 'Thank goodness! For a horrible moment there I thought you might have gone already.'

'Almost.' Beth was dressed in a pair of jeans and a soft, comfortable-looking sweatshirt. 'Brent's gone to find a taxi and Mum's dishing out all the flowers to the other patients. They'll be back in a minute, I expect.'

'Oh…' Luke held Beth's gaze and was suddenly tongue-tied. So she was intending to leave, then. There was too much to try and say and not nearly enough time. Beth's eyes looked too big and dark for her pale face and she looked…miserable. Luke couldn't interpret her expression. Did she now want him to be here?

'How are you feeling?'

'A lot better.' Beth's head dipped and Luke could see her blinking. Hard. As though she was struggling not to cry.

Luke stepped closer to the armchair, intending to crouch and get on the same level as Beth. It wouldn't be so easy for her to avoid eye contact that way. And he would be close enough to touch her.

The movement was arrested halfway, however, by

the glimpse that getting to the window afforded. A taxi was parked near Ocean View's front door. Brent Granger was talking to the driver. He tapped his watch and then pointed up at the building, and Luke found himself stepping back.

Had Brent seen him?

Did it matter?

Hell, yes. It would be less than a couple of minutes before Brent swept into Beth's room and tried to assume control. If he'd seen Luke, he would be able to halve that length of time.

'Beth!' Luke did drop to a crouch now and his tone was urgent. 'I really need to talk to you.'

Her face was so much thinner and there were dark shadows under her eyes. She looked so tired. It would hardly be fair for him and Brent to stand in front of her, competing in any way for the right to take care of her.

But she was saying nothing. Just staring at him…waiting for *him* to say something else.

And there was too much to say and the clock was ticking mercilessly.

'Do you *want* to go away with Brent?'

The question came out more abruptly than Luke had intended. Was that why Beth hesitated? Why the head was slow enough to give the impression of uncertainty? Luke deliberately softened his tone.

'Would *you* like to talk, Beth?'

A nod this time, but the glance towards the door reminded Luke of how impossible a deeply personal discussion would become in a very short space of time.

'Right.' For the first time in far too long Luke suddenly felt in total control. Strong. Invincible even. He slipped an arm behind Beth and the other under her knees. 'Hang on,' he instructed.

She squeaked, but it didn't sound as though Luke had hurt her by lifting her out of the armchair.

'What *are* you doing, Luke?'

'Taking you somewhere we can talk,' Luke said grimly. 'By ourselves.'

He smiled at the face so close to his own and Beth closed her eyes and rested her head on his shoulder.

'Oh…' she murmured. 'That's good.'

A startled group of nurses, including Roz from emergency, made way for his determined progress towards the exit once they reached the ground floor.

'What's happened?' Roz gasped. 'Is Beth all right?'

'She will be,' Luke called back over his shoulder. 'I intend to make sure of that.'

He shoved the fire-stop doors open with his shoulder and managed to keep holding Beth as he opened the passenger door on the Jeep. Depositing her gently onto the seat, he did up her safety belt then frowned.

'Are you OK? Nothing hurting?'

'I'm fine. Where are we going?'

'You'll see.' Luke smiled and then shut the door. After opening the driver's door, he glanced back at the main hospital building. His gaze tracked upwards and he was not surprised to see faces staring down from what had been Beth's window.

One of those faces was that of Brent Granger, and even from this distance Luke could sense his fury.

He raised his hand in a somewhat dismissive salute and found he was grinning as he flicked the key in the ignition and gunned the engine of his powerful vehicle.

This was it.

His chance.

And he was going to do whatever it might take to succeed.

The bumps in the shingle road that led down to Boulder Bay beach were enough to jar Beth's healing abdominal incision, but the pain in no way burst the bubble of joy inside her.

She had come so close to giving up on Luke. Sitting in that armchair and waiting for Brent to come and take her to the waiting taxi, Beth had decided that Luke was not coming back. He wasn't bothered by the fact that Brent had come back to try and lay claim to her future. Maybe he had even been relieved.

But he *had* come. And it hadn't been just to say goodbye. Beth had watched his face as he'd looked at her empty bed. It had been so hard not to just dissolve into tears when she had seen the miraculous change of expression and heard that heartfelt sigh of relief when she had spoken. She still felt unbelievably weak and her own relief, on top of the misery that Luke's continuing absence had fed, had been overwhelming.

So overwhelming it had been too much to try and take in. Until she had seen the hope that flared in Luke's eyes. Her own response had been so powerful that Beth had actually wondered if a heart could break from such a sudden rush of so much love.

What was it that had held her back from saying something then? Something that would convince her that this time it *would* work? That she could offer all the love she still had for Luke—and more—and it wouldn't end in heartbreak?

Of course she didn't want to go away with Brent and

of course she wanted to talk. But Beth had wanted to listen even more at that moment so she'd stayed silent, simply shaking and then nodding her head. Until the surprise of being scooped up into Luke's arms.

She hadn't cared where he was taking her. She hadn't cared how long it would take. With her arms around Luke's neck and her head in the comfortable dip just below his shoulder, Beth would have been perfectly happy to have been carried to the ends of the earth.

Mind you, Boulder Bay was the perfect end to what seemed like a very long journey. One that had taken six years, in fact.

'Are you feeling all right?' Luke was peering at Beth anxiously as he traced the outline of her cheekbone with a fingertip.

'A bit tired,' Beth admitted. She smiled. 'Must be all the excitement of being abducted.'

'Do you want to stay where you are?' Luke turned to scan the beach. 'We've got the place to ourselves if you'd like to sit on the sand somewhere.'

'I'd love to feel the sun,' Beth nodded. 'And to smell the sea. It feels like I've been shut away for rather a long time.'

Luke carried her again. He took off the soft leather jacket he was wearing and padded it to make a cushion against the smooth side of a boulder. Beth sank onto the warmth of the sand and sighed happily.

'This is perfect.'

'A bit different from the last time we were here.' Luke's smile was almost smug. 'We're all alone.'

He was giving her *that* look. The one that said she was the only thing of any importance in the universe as far as he was concerned. The one that meant he wanted to kiss her and would do so if she gave him the slightest indication that his touch would be welcome.

Beth's mouth felt suddenly dry and her heart skipped a beat. She wasn't ready. Not quite yet.

Beth looked around at the gentle waves washing onto pristine sand amongst smooth boulders. 'What happened to the other whales? The ones that didn't make it?'

'They've been taken away. Buried.' Luke knelt on the sand beside Beth and took hold of one of her hands. He caught Beth's gaze and held it. His mouth opened then closed and then he cleared his throat. His smile was embarrassed.

'I've got so much to say I don't know where to start.'

'Try the beginning,' Beth suggested helpfully.

'Do you want the long version or the short version?'

'How short is the short version?'

'Very short.' Any hint of amusement died from Luke's face and his features settled into lines serious enough to alarm Beth.

'Three words, Beth,' Luke said softly. 'I love you.'

She could feel the words just as clearly as she could hear them. They enfolded her in warmth and the bubble of joy inside her was overfull. Little bits of that joy were leaking into Beth's bloodstream and sending the most delicious tingles into every cell in her body.

'I love you, too, Luke,' she whispered.

His face moved closer, his lips on their way to claim hers, but Beth raised her hand and pressed her fingertips against the softness of those lips.

'Now I want to hear the long version.'

Luke groaned softly.

'Please?'

Beth could see Luke collect himself and had to hide a smile of secret joy that it was clearly so difficult to rein in the desire to kiss her. She wanted that kiss just as much as he did but she knew that it would be worth waiting for. That it would be even better when she knew the answers to those questions that had provided such a puzzle. Luke nodded slowly, as though he understood and agreed. He didn't let go of Beth's hand but he sat back to lean on the boulder beside her and he trapped that hand between both of his own. Then he sighed softly.

'I was at a funeral this morning, Beth.'

'Oh…that's awful!' How selfish had she been— deciding that if Luke cared about her he would have been there at the hospital with her? Beth searched Luke's face anxiously. 'Was it someone close?'

Luke nodded solemnly. 'As close as it's possible to get.'

Beth could feel her eyes widening. A *woman*? But Luke's smile was reassuring.

'Without sex, of course.' He squeezed her hand. 'Kev was my best mate. We grew up together. He and my twin sister, Jodie, fell in love at high school and they got married a year later after I left Auckland. When I was living in Wellington after…after…'

After his relationship with *her* had ended. Beth returned the hand squeeze and nodded to encourage Luke to continue and not get sidetracked by ground they didn't need to revisit.

'They were so in love,' Luke said wistfully. 'And they had so much to look forward to. They spent three months backpacking in Europe for a honeymoon and then Jodie got a job at Ocean View as a physiotherapist and Kev's electronic business started taking off. They were talking about trying for a baby just before their first anniversary and then…Jodie got sick.'

Luke closed his eyes for a second and when he spoke again it seemed that his professional tone was a deliberate attempt to keep still raw emotions in check.

'It was leukaemia. Acute myeloid. For a long time we thought we could beat it. I was a near perfect match as a donor, thanks to being a twin, I guess, so I had bone marrow harvested twice. I would have done it again. Hell, I would have donated any part of my body that might have done the trick, but we didn't get the chance to try again. She died four years ago when she was only thirty-two years old.'

'Oh…*Luke*!' Beth ignored the tears she could feel trickling down her cheeks. 'I'm *so* sorry.'

'Yeah.' Luke's attempt at a smile was heart-wrenching. 'I know. Anyway, I spent as much time as I could with her over that year she was sick. My job suffered with all the time I took off, but it didn't seem to matter. I just didn't really care any more. About anything. It felt like the bottom had dropped out of my world. My parents and Kev were just as devastated, of course, so I kept coming back to spend time with them. We helped each other get through it and about six months later I realised I didn't want to be anywhere else. I took only as much time as I needed to complete my training as a general surgeon and then I moved to Hereford and bought this place.'

'I wish I could have been here to help.'

'It's just as well you weren't.'

'Why do you say that?'

'Because if I'd had you to lean on, I would have found it so much easier to cope. I would have built a bridge of some kind and just kept going the same way I had been. You *were* right, you know. About why you doubted our future together. I would have ended up like your father,' Luke confessed. 'I was on the same track back then, wasn't I? And I never saw it. When Jodie died I learned something. Something I suspect you knew all along.' His smile was gentle enough to bring fresh tears to Beth's eyes.

'What was that?'

'It doesn't matter how much money or prestige or power you get in life,' Luke said quietly. 'None of it matters a damn when you're dying. The only thing that counts then is being with the people you love. The people that love you.'

Luke's gaze told Beth that *she* was the person he loved. His smile was another caress.

'They say life is for living, don't they? But I reckon they're wrong. Life is for *loving*. And the more you give, the more you get back.'

Beth could only nod. No words could have made it past that lump in her throat.

'Sometimes,' Luke continued, 'if you're lucky, you find a love that's so powerful it outshines any other. Kev found that kind of love with Jodie.' Luke's voice caught and thickened. 'He told me he wasn't afraid to die, Beth. And I can understand that now.'

'You can? But he was so young! It's tragic.'

Luke nodded slowly. Then he took his hands away from Beth's so that he could cradle her face.

'A love like that is so strong that even dying isn't something to be afraid of. It's living without that person that causes the fear.' A tiny tremor was transmitted from the hands holding Beth's face. 'And that, Elizabeth Dawson, is the kind of love I have for you.' Luke's thumbs moved to brush the last traces of tears from Beth's cheeks and then follow the outline of her lips. 'I'm afraid to live without you.'

'I'm not going anywhere, Luke,' Beth whispered. 'I feel exactly the same way about you.'

'You don't have to say that.' Luke drew Beth into his arms and held her so close she could feel every beat of his heart. He kissed her softly. 'You're still nowhere near well. You're vulnerable right now. I just had to make sure you knew how *I* felt before you went away anywhere.'

'I'm not going anywhere,' Beth repeated. 'And I might be a bit wobbly but that doesn't change how I feel, Luke. I knew the first day I saw you again that I could never leave. That…that I still loved you.'

Luke kissed her again. 'How did you know that?'

'You told me I was brilliant.' The memory of that spark and her attempts to talk herself out of giving it any significance made Beth smile. 'I realised that what you thought was more important than anything anyone else could ever think.'

'What about…?' Luke's hesitation was palpable. 'Brent?'

'I don't love Brent. he knows that. Yes, I dated him for a while. And I was very lonely after Neroli had gone to Australia. I was down enough to start thinking I would never find what I really wanted in life and I might miss out completely if I couldn't compromise in some way. It wasn't until Brent talked me into accepting his proposal that I realised that what had attracted me to him were only the things that reminded me of you. It would have been dishonest to let it go any further and I told him that.' Beth shook her head. 'I only wore that ring for a week and then I gave it back to him and explained why we could never be married. I haven't even spoken to him since.'

'He's not going to be happy.'

'I wasn't going back to Auckland because he wanted me to,' Beth assured Luke. 'I knew I wasn't going to be much use for anything around here for a while and it would be nice to spend some time with my Mum.'

'I've got a mum,' Luke said proudly. 'She's very good at looking after things. Gardens, people...whales. You name it.'

'I couldn't land myself on your mum. Especially right now. Maybe I could just stay in hospital for another day or two.'

'And then go back to that motel? I don't think so.' Luke kissed Beth again, rather firmly this time. 'I'll take you back to both those places very soon. We'll stop at Kev's house on the way so I can tell Mum what's happening.'

Beth turned her face up so that she could receive another kiss. 'What *is* happening?'

'A new beginning.' Luke smiled. 'You were right about something else, you know.'

'What?'

'You're not going anywhere. After you've had a chat to Brent and we collect all your things from the hospital and the motel, you're coming home with me. I'm going to be the one looking after you from now on.' The anxious look that followed such a firm declaration was almost comical. 'That is, if that's what *you* want, hon.'

Beth snuggled back into Luke's embrace. 'It's what I want,' she confirmed happily. 'Can you cook?'

'Of course I can cook.'

'You don't sound very sure about that.'

'Doesn't matter, anyway. My mum makes the best casseroles you've ever tasted. She can give me some lessons.'

Beth pulled back far enough to beam at Luke. 'That's great!'

'Why? Can't you cook either?'

'Of course I can cook. It's just that I've got this really nice casserole dish that needs christening.'

Luke shook his head in fond bewilderment. Then he kissed Beth yet again before levering himself into a position from which he could gather her up into his arms.

'Come on, then. We need to get ourselves organised.'

'For cooking?' Beth was feeling weary enough to simply let the joy of being with Luke be the only thought she needed to hold.

'No,' Luke said sternly. 'For spending the rest of our lives together.'

'Oh…' Beth wrapped her arms more tightly around the nec of the man she loved. 'What are we waiting for, then?'

'Just this.'

Luke bent his head and kissed her…again.

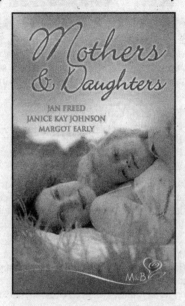